RECTIFY
The Avenging Angel

Ryan J. Russell

DEDICATION

I dedicate this book to my parents, especially my mother, who has given more to me than I will ever know.

Second, I dedicate this book to the person who inspired the character of Sonya and all who have suffered from similar crimes.

Third, I plan to dedicate 10% of all proceeds to Operation Underground Railroad to aid in their work of rescuing children and stopping those involved in the sex and slave trade.

Fourth, this book is dedicated to all those who have risked their lives, protecting the innocent, and doing what they were called on to do. I acknowledge the sacrifices of those who came home and those who didn't. All leave something behind; those who return suffer in many ways. Don't struggle alone. Help is out there.

CONTENTS

PROLOGUE

Somewhere beyond the earth, by a power no mortal can comprehend, two prayers were heard, as are all sincere pleas. Many prayers are answered, but in the case of Dan Campbell and Paul Gutierrez, not the way they hoped.

Both were known very well by this All-Mighty Being, who knew them better than they knew themselves. He had known them before they submitted themselves to mortality. He knew the dreams and wants that in despair, both had forgotten. Neither prayer was selfish, and both offered for another; with so much faith and fervor, they could not be denied. As the one who sent them to face mortality and knew their true nature, He knew what they wanted before they asked. He had long known this day would come. Both prayers would be answered, but in a way, neither man would have asked for, had he known the way they would be answered.

Long had the halls of eternity prepared for this moment, with only a

1

thought, a message was sent to another. "He will be here soon." Then turning his attention back to the two men, he sorrowed for the heartache they would face for a moment, then smiled, for he saw the day when both would receive what they wanted and deserved.

CHAPTER 1
DYING

Major Dan Campbell, one of the deadliest men in the world, was dying.

But at least he went out the way a warrior should, in an Afghani warlords'

compound, surrounded by dead terrorists. The good news was his mission

was a success, a human trafficker was dead, and many girls had been saved

from the horrors of sex trafficking. It was getting hard to see, but he could

hear his men rushing towards him.

"Campbell, that was amazing, but why didn't you wait?" The

breathless voice of his second-in-command Paul Gutierrez shouted as he

ran towards his friend.

They were doing their best to patch him up, but when you've been shot in

the gut, hours away from the nearest medical facility, there's not much

anyone can do to save you.

Dan knew he was dying; he had to laugh a little on the inside. He had imagined being a Navy Seal all his life, he achieved that dream. Now here

he was, a Delta Force Operative dying after an engagement, the world

would never know about.

He thought back on that fateful day when Delta Force came recruiting, he

couldn't refuse. They promoted him to the rank of Major several years early

and gave him a task force charged with stopping human trafficking,

specifically sex trafficking. They knew he couldn't say no. Everyone in the

Special Forces community knew how adamant he was about preventing

sexual abuse and saving others from the trauma faced by the only girl he

had ever loved. She continued to suffer from PTSD caused by the trauma

of being raped at a young age and other sexual abuse she lived through

before she met Dan.

The military could have given him the rank of Private and he still would

have accepted the offer. He did not mind the pay increase; it meant he

could spend more on his own work, under the nickname his men gave him.

A smile crept across his face. If someone were to put a price tag on training;

he was possibly the most expensive soldier in the history of the United

States, perhaps the world. He had killed men on six continents, three

oceans, and saved thousands from slavery or worse. It's hard to stay

humble when you think you're untouchable. Dan would comfortably say

that no man could kill him, only a mistake on his part would. Unfortunately, today the mistake happened; at least he was right about no man being able to kill him…

Hesitation was his mistake. He had never hesitated to kill a man before, but a 12-year-old boy, trying to avenge his father, that had never happened before. Just a few seconds of hesitation was now the cause of his death. Dan could not blame the boy; he would have done the same thing if he saw someone kill his father.

The events leading up to this moment replayed in his mind. He and his men had been waiting in the hills of northern Afghanistan for several nights. It seemed more like 2 months as they waited for the non-combat personnel to show up and orders to be received. One of Dan's favorite parts of being a Delta Force Operative was the autonomy and being somewhat free to act of their own accord in the field. But not today! One of the men spotted the non-coms on the road headed for their location.

It's about time, Dan thought to himself. It took every ounce of patience Dan possessed to wait this long. He could have had the girls rescued, Aco and his whole operation destroyed, and been sleeping in a barracks tonight, but politicians got involved. He jogged over to the radio; sure, they would let him engage now that the non-coms were within view.

Shaking his head and rolling his shoulders to hide his anger, he hit the transmit button

"Kermit to Pond, request permission to engage? Non-coms are in sight."

He didn't like the call sign Kermit, but when you're an ex-seal working in the Army, it's almost expected, it could've been a lot worse.

The radio crackled.

"Negative, do not engage until support arrives."

Clenching his jaw to control his growing anger, he stayed silent for the time it took him to gain composure. Over his career, Dan used his degree in psychology to help hundreds of trafficked victims. He knew he could help the girls in need of rescue with the psychological trauma associated with trafficking. He didn't need some UN Social Workers and their escorts getting in the way. He had to remind himself that he was still a soldier, subject to following orders.

He may not have voted for the new president, but he was still the Commander and Chief. When he or she gives an order, you obey. Under the previous administration, Dan had been allowed to run things as he saw fit because that president let the military do their job. However, right now, all the wishing in the world wouldn't change anything. It was early September 2012, so maybe this coming election would bring someone to the office more military-minded. But then even if the unthinkable happened and the current president got re-elected; he wouldn't leave Americans or military personnel without all possible help.

Shaking his head, he returned his focus to the mission as he gazed over the compound of Zaman Aco. He had been chasing this scum of a human being for 3 years! Aco destroyed the lives of so many young women and their families; it made Dan sick inside. Three weeks ago, Aco abducted 30 teenage girls and planned to sell them to the highest bidders. Dan was ready to strike as soon as the details were learned, but somehow the United Nations found out and were given permission to interfere in his work. Oh, how he hated politicians! *Someone was probably covering something up.* Dan thought to himself. He hoped someday to rectify that and make all dirty politicians pay.

A truck entering the compound, grabbed his attention. It's speed indicated it was empty and ready to be loaded with the girls. They would be taken to an auction where they would be exposed to untold horrors. They had stopped many of Aco's operations, killing lieutenants and critical people in his infrastructure. Still, they had never been able to catch him. No matter who was killed, there always seemed to be more tendrils to his operation. Of the few men they captured, all were too frightened to talk. Aco only put men with families in leadership positions, and if any talked, their families would be killed. These men fought like lions and did all they could to avoid capture, but Dan Campbell was hard to shake.

Despite all his cautions, Aco made a mistake. Dan couldn't help but smile because Aco's mistake had been calling a man's mother a whore. No matter how non-threatening a person may seem, you don't insult their mother.

Hoping he had given himself enough time to calm down, he once again picked the radio up.

"Kermit to Pond. It's now, or never! The girls are about to be loaded on a truck. If we do not strike now, we will lose them!"

"Hold position, additional personnel ETA 30 minutes. Do not engage, repeat do not engage."

It was all he could do not to slam the radio to the ground. If they didn't start their attack within the next five minutes, he knew it would be too late. He hated dealing with bureaucrats, if he were in charge, they would already be engaged, instead, they were stuck waiting for blue-helmeted babysitters. He had spoken to several UN soldiers during his military career. Most of them were good soldiers, but their orders stank of bureaucracy.

"LISTEN… I mean…Pond." He forced a smile and spoke through clenched teeth. "If we do not engage in five minutes, the girls are gone. Please verify!" He said it calmly but in a clearly angry tone.

"Kermit, you have your orders! Do not engage, additional staff must be present, your unit is not to engage until additional personnel arrives."

He slammed the radio down! For someone who didn't swear, he was thinking some nasty things. Punching his hand with his fist, he imagined it was whatever bureaucrat was interfering with his work.

From behind him, Dan heard, "So, what are we going to do, boss?"

Dan turned to see his second-in-command Lieutenant Paul Gutierrez, more than just second-in-command; he was the closest thing to a friend Dan had these days. Turning, Dan stood and faced his friend who stood a few inches taller than his 5 foot 11 inches. Despite having gone to a military academy, Dan had to respect his friend, who was everything an officer should be.

As a new Major in Delta force, Dan had been deeply impressed by Sergeant First Class Paul Gutierrez. Dan always jokingly said Paul should have joined the Navy because he was too smart for the Army, to which Paul always replied, guess they figured out their mistake and sent you to the Army. The respect wasn't simply because of his knowledge of war and soldiers, or that he was one of the best all-around fighters Dan had ever seen. No, it was because Dan saw a man born to lead, and at his pushing, Paul had done the work and was now a 33-year-old First Lieutenant a year older than Dan.

"Orders are orders," Dan said, shrugging with a straight face. "Take the unit and wait for the UN idiots. Hold position until support arrives. I'm… going forward to observe. Join me when they arrive so we can move out when the order comes in."

Paul took a few steps then turned back. "Dan? You're not going to do something stupid, are you?"

Dan smiled. "Well, I did join the Army!" He said with a wink and a laugh. "I'm just going to observe; don't worry, I'll do what's right. But when this is over, I'm going to find whoever was behind this mess, and knock him into next week."

Paul had a sense of foreboding in his gut, something wasn't right, but he couldn't place what it was. "OK" He smiled unconvincingly and hesitantly turned away. "But you know we will do whatever you say, right? Every man in this unit will follow you."

"Yeah man, I know. Thank you, brother! You have followed me into hell. No doubt with you and the men at my back, we would have the world cleared out of terrorists in a week." Dan said with his trademark smile.

Paul saluted as crisply as a Private out of boot camp. "Yes, Sir," followed immediately by a wink, and briskly walked to the other men. He could tell his friend was in a sour mood and needed to chill out; he just needed time and space.

"Ha, real funny ya moron," Dan called out after Paul for his exaggerated formality.

Even after 3 years in the Army, Dan wasn't sure he would ever get used to hearing "yes sir" instead of "aye-aye." However, such formality wasn't usually followed by his men; it was understood that when a command was given, they followed. He hoped for their sakes they obeyed his last order.

Checking to make sure none of the men saw him, Dan grabbed his gear and started toward the enemy compound. Better to ask for forgiveness than permission. He wasn't about to let these teenage girls be sold into who knows what. Had he been allowed his usual freedom to operate, he could have taken the compound with a troop of Boy Scouts.

Looking over the shallow valley, a slight cool breeze was blowing dust about in the early evening light, made darker by a blanket of gray clouds. Having grown up in Southeastern Arizona, the sight of dust and the sound of it blowing was comforting. The similarities ended there. This dust didn't smell like home. It may have looked similar, but smelled like a blend of burning goat hair, feces, and gunpowder, from the years of warfare and human atrocities.

Before clearing the rise hiding their position, Dan planted the butt of his rifle on the ground. He wrapped his hands around the barrel like a knight with his sword and said a quick prayer. He then felt the knife at his side and thought of the one who gave it to him as he always did before heading out. He didn't feel as comfortable as he had on previous missions. A sense of foreboding filled his gut, as he moved towards the compoud. He was the only hope for those girls and knew he had to act.

*

Dan was within the engagement zone when Paul returned to check the status, but there was no sign of Campbell. A frantic voice crackled on the discarded radio calling for Kermit. Instantly he knew what Campbell had done and cursed himself for not listening to his gut. It wasn't the first time Campbell had done something like this; he just hoped, as usual, it wasn't the last.

Cursing under his breath, Paul quickly clicked on his comms. "Grab your gear!"

He answered the radio, in his best Campbell voice, "Receiving, over!"

"New intel, engage immediately, the target is in motion!"

"Son of a... Roger!"

Clicking on his direct comms. "Campbell, you idiot, what are you doing!?" But he received no answer, Dan had turned his comms off so his men wouldn't come with him.

The rest of the men, hearing a string of profanity, came running to see what was wrong because they all knew Campbell felt strongly about profanity and the men respected him enough to try and control their language in his presence. He would blow off or ignore an occasional slip. If it was more, he just gave a look. If one of his men were hurt, he would tolerate them saying whatever was needed to help with the pain. However, no one was hurt, so they immediately knew something was wrong. Seeing an angry Gutierrez throwing the radio down and no Campbell, a collective "ugh" sounded with a few, "not again" comments mixed in. Paul and the rest of the men moved out immediately to support their leader, despite their irritation with him. He could be impetuous and cocky, he still had their total support, and though none would admit it, he was the soldier they all aspired to be.

In the distance, barely visible in the waning light, they could see their commander, the size of an action figure crouching behind a bush waiting for a patrol to pass.

*

The enemy left a significant gap in their perimeter, which Dan took full advantage of. Today he was grateful for the heavy cover offered by the rain-filled clouds, giving him a hiding place behind each rock and bush. The enemy's patrol points and timing were memorized. After a brief wait, he did what he always did. Try to turn his feelings off and tell himself that he was not fighting humans.

The things he was fighting today were not human. Anything standing between him and rescuing the girls would have to die. Anyone who worked for a man like Aco could not be human. If somehow, they had no choice in the matter, then they would surrender rather than fight.

He heard the footsteps at least 15 seconds before the first contact came into view. With the enemy's back to him, he leapt up, stabbed his knife into the side of the man's neck, sawing forward, the man quickly bled out. It was bloody work, but was no different than a lion on the savanna taking down a gazelle. Today Dan was the lion, and this was his first prey of the day. He knew later it would bother him as he washed the blood from his fatigues, but those thoughts were quickly pushed out of his mind.

Wiping his knife on the back of the scum who had just been killed, Dan moved on. When he wasn't in combat, everyone was human, but in war, it's much easier to kill if they aren't human. He did his best to keep a separation between his civilian and warrior self. Civilian Dan Campbell hated killing and looked forward to the day when he wouldn't have to. Warrior Dan Campbell did it because he had to and he was good at it, more than just a soldier. When he was in his element, he liked to think of himself by the nickname his men and enemies had bestowed upon him, The Avenging Angel.

He didn't have time to hide the body; he just had to hope it wouldn't be discovered until his work was done. At some point, he knew his men would get the order to advance. They would know what to do with the bodies he left behind. He silently killed two more with his knife, but the sound of a truck starting in the distance spurred him to hurry. He had to become careless, which was when mistakes happened. The knife was taking too long, he would have to break basic special ops rules. He had always been lucky, so why not today?

He found himself on a slight rise overlooking the compound, there had to be more than three pickets in the area, but he or his men would have to deal with them later. On the four corners of the compound were guard towers. Taking out his rifle, he gulped, marked his first target, and pulled the trigger. That one shot ringing out in the night began an endless cacophony of mayhem.

*

Paul and the rest of the unit were halfway to the compound when the evening's silence was pierced by the sound of one shot, followed by more gunshots and then the sirens. Paul's heart lurched in his chest.

Campbell, what are you doing? If this doesn't kill you, I just might do it myself, he thought to himself.

Clicking his comms back on, Paul again tried to reach Campbell with no answer and no orders. These men were Delta Force, they didn't need to be commanded, and each man knew what he had to do. They automatically double-timed to the campound, each man hoping they got to Campbell in time. They ran past the first lifeless bodies and continued forward, never losing a step, their minds focused on getting to that compound where Campbell had unleashed the horrors of hell.

Paul reflected on his friend. *When not in combat, there wasn't a kinder person than Dan, but he had no equal on the battlefield. When Dan Campbell fought to defend the weak, or for a cause he believed in, he had no fear. Each man admired Dan, and they cared for him as much as he cared for those girls. But secretly, they all felt sorrow for him because he loved a woman that could never love him the same way he loved her. None felt that sorrow for Campbell as much as Paul Gutierrez. He had a wife and children to go home to. It always broke his heart whenever Campbell visited, and Paul saw the longing in his eyes for the same kind of life with Sonya. The way Dan talked about her, in fact, everything he did, including this stupid move, was because he loved her. Though Dan never would have admitted it, Paul had a suspicion that every man Campbell killed to rescue a woman was paying for the one who raped Sonya.*

Paul shook his head to get his mind back on the fight. He had to get Campbell through this; he just had to. Campbell might've been the Avenging Angel and one of the deadliest men in the world, but deep down, he never should've been here. Dan had a plan. He was going to finish his military career and then settle down with Sonya, even if it was just as a friend. Still, Paul knew he wanted marriage and a life with her. Paul took off running. It probably wouldn't work, but if any man deserved a chance for that life, it was Dan Campbell. Campbell always prayed before every mission, so Paul figured he should try, though he couldn't remember how, and was sure God wouldn't expect to hear from him. Never stopping, Paul thought a simple soldier's prayer.

God, I don't know if you're listening. Please just get Campbell through this. He deserves a chance at true love.

*

Dan cleared the first two corner guard towers, hitting each man twice. The whole compound was on alert; men ran out of every building to fight, still unsure of where exactly the bullets were coming from. He took out the other two tower guards, then hearing footsteps behind him, slid down the 8-foot slope to the level of the compound, rolled to his knee, turned, and killed the man who had been behind him. Turning back, he shot a man standing in front of the building's double doors, who had been so surprised, he died before even bringing his rifle to bear. Dan's training was so exact and precise, he didn't have to think; his body just reacted.

In the adrenaline high, he didn't even notice the pain in his knee, making him limp. With his gun level, he kicked the door in, instantly putting down three men standing in the courtyard. He hoped the girls were still inside, as he entered the building from the square. It appeared most of the men had been cleared from the inner courtyard, meaning the others must be outside loading the truck. He found the door to the cells, but they were empty: The smell of human feces was a testament to the treatment the girls endured. Running to the front gate, there were two men waiting for him. He shot one, the other fired before he could put him down, the bullet grazing his abdomen. His body armor had paid off today

Other gunshots came in his direction, forcing him to dive behind a low wall. Then there was a moment of silence, which was probably only a few seconds, but it felt more like two minutes after all the noise. The silence was broken by a man shouting in heavily accented broken English for him to give up. Of course, they wanted him to surrender, he would go for a high price, many would pay a king's ransom for a United States Special Forces Officer. That price would quadruple if they discovered he was the Avenging Angel. He half smirked at the thought of how his men's nickname for him had spread amongst their enemies. Indeed, they knew he wouldn't surrender, but when someone is afraid for their life, they'll take any chance they can get.

Suddenly shots came from behind Dan, killing the men in front of him, and he heard others firing in the distance. His men had come. He switched on his headset, to the sound of Paul repeating his name over and over.

"I thought I told you to stay back! What are you doing here?"

"What!? We're here to save your sorry… er butt. Now listen! Those… uh, forward command gave the go-ahead! Stay low. You've got combatants coming from all sides, but we can maintain, be there shortly, just wait for us. Okay?"

"Those girls don't have that kind of time," Dan replied. "The truck has started, and they're already loading 'em."

Dan popped up, killing two more men. He saw the headlights of the truck in the distance and heard muffled cries. He offered a short silent prayer.

THE AVENGING ANGEL

If you just let me save these girls, I will serve you; however, you see fit.

Even in the middle of combat, he felt a momentary calm and a chill travel through his body. Evidently, his prayer had been heard. He smiled at the assurance he wouldn't die today.

Dan was aware of 2 to 4 men in front of him, but he would use the element of surprise and do something they might have expected only in a Chuck Norris movie. Replacing his magazine and making a mental count of his remaining ammo, he popped up and fired, making short work of the first two men. He continued forward, passing a building, judging by the smell, was an outhouse, another man stood from behind cover and managed to hit him with two rounds center mass. Slamming Dan against the outhouse wall, dazing him for a few seconds. His training took over, his body automatically responding. Luckily, the man hadn't checked his ammo and was searching for another magazine for his ancient assault rifle. Dan recovered instantly, not even noticing the few broken ribs and internal bruising he for sure had. Now it was his turn to fire two rounds at the man. Both hit, killing him instantly. He watched two men near the truck fall. He was going to have to thank someone for those two. Instead of trying to run or surrender, the driver reached for a shotgun on the dash, until a shot through the passenger window stopped him.

The girls were on the ground at the back of the truck. One pointed to a building at the front of the truck, at the same moment, he heard 4 o'clock over the radio. He turned to see seven men running out of the building towards him, only 20 feet away. He emptied his magazine, killing the first four, his men killed two others, leaving just one running towards him with a knife. Out of ammo, he threw his empty rifle at the man throwing his momentum off enough that he was able to position himself to intercept. When the man reached him and brought the knife down. Dan was able to stop his downward motion, not even noticing the deep slash he took on the arm or the dripping blood. Without thinking, Dan used his enemy's momentum to slam him into the truck, with a grunt and the sound of the metal door being smashed in. The force was so hard that it knocked the knife to the ground.

Dan tried to hit him in the eye with his left elbow before the man could react but missed and only cut his eyebrow open. Holding him up with his right forearm pressed against his chest, all thoughts of proper technique were replaced by brutal survival instinct. With a knee to the man's groin, he let him drop to the ground. Some of his senses restored, Dan looked into the face and almost laughed at the sight looking up at him.

As if it were some Hollywood movie, he stared into the face of evil. Though half concealed by blood running from his eyebrow, it was the cruelest sex trafficker in Afghanistan, if not the world, Zaman Aco. Dan never felt so revolted in all his life. As he looked into Acos eyes, and saw pure evil, a foul shudder went down Dan's spine. It made his blood boil that he even had to touch this thing.

With his one eye rendered useless by the blood running into it, and the blood spluttering off his lips when he spoke, Aco begged for mercy. Dan reached down and picked up the knife. He had been hunting Aco for years; he wanted nothing more than to beat him to death for all the evil he had caused. On Dan's bedroom wall was the face of every known victim of this man. He promised them every day, he would bring them justice. Now was his chance; the only thing stopping him was the spirit within him, screaming for him to stop or risk becoming what he hated.

In his mind, a voice said, *Vengeance is mine. This will not bring you or them, peace.* The struggle to control his anger was such a strain for his body that tears began to fall. No, he would not make Aco suffer no matter how much he wanted to, but he still didn't drop the knife as an idea hit him.

Knowing the creature below him spoke English, he looked into those hollow, evil eyes one clouded by blood and said through a clenched jaw.

"You want mercy? I can take you in alive or dead. Why shouldn't I kill you?"

Dan pushed his hand against the man's neck, applying pressure, his cut arm burning from the effort. Aco quickly tried to answer, fear for his life evident in his one open eye.

Gaining more composure, Dan loosened his grasp on the man's neck by a slight degree. Tempted to let him live, in case he could lead them to others.

Facing death and thinking Dan was just another soft, greedy American, Aco figured he would be persuaded by greed and pity.

"Please spare my life, let me go, and I'll never do this again. I will give you anything in my possession, I will give you money, diamonds, gold, women. Let me go, and anything you want is yours."

That was when Dan Campbell made his decision. He didn't care what happened anymore. He knew his next action could possibly be the end of his career, but this was an offer he couldn't refuse. His body shook from barely controlled rage, but never diverting his eyes, Dan replied with a half-smile half sneer crossing his face.

"Anything I want?" Dan asked, his voice rising as though he were sincerely interested. "Hmm… money, women… Yes," rubbing his chin in thought with his knife-hand. "Oh," he said as though he had just had a brilliant idea, "yes, I'll let you go for women… and money." A quick look of relief and knowing crossed Aco's face; in his experience, any man could be bought, especially with women and money.

An audible "WHAT THE!" sounded in his ear from Paul on the radio before Dan cut him off with more words.

"How about you give me every woman, or girl you've ever sold into slavery and all who have died, and mourned because of you? Return those daughters and mothers to their families. Undue all the evil you have done! Do that, and I'll let you live!"

Fear filled the man's eye as he just stared blankly up at Dan.

"Coward!" Dan said in disgust. "But I'm not going to kill you, I will let you live."

Aco eased for a moment, shocked at his fortune, but tormented by the stress of waffling between life and death. He was not surprised because these sheltered spoiled Americans were soft, or so he thought. His prejudices were proven false when Dan again pushed on his neck and raised the knife, turning it and looking at it as though trying to decipher some secret it held. The thing, which some would call a man, looked at it terrified as a puddle of yellow liquid pooled beneath him.

Dan looked back into Aco's one open eye. "This knife is a Marine's weapon, and you don't look like a Marine to me, the only way a Marine gives up his weapon is if he's dead. So, it's not me killing you, the Marine who owned this Ka-bar is killing you, I'm just the delivery boy." He said grimly.

Thoughts of the brutalized corpses Aco and his men had left behind, made the beast inside Dan beg to torture Aco. He couldn't deny; he had imagined it many times and wondered if he could. He probably could if it were to find a family member or to save lives, but what good would it do here. Many thoughts went through his head, *what would he do if Jesus was standing next to him, he wouldn't condone torture just for vengeance? What would his mother think? He didn't think she would object to the death of Aco either, but what would she think, knowing that her son could torture a man out of hatred? He had already been through and done things he never wanted her to know, but how could he even look at her knowing he had done it?*

Then he thought of Sonya: At first, he thought, *I could kill Aco for her.* Then a realization struck him; *after what she had experienced, why would she want more violence?* He had felt the same feeling before that she needed peace, yet he was going around the world, killing to protect and save others in her honor. *How could that be wrong? It wasn't necessarily wrong, but was it right? He was able to kill in combat, and when it was to save lives, it didn't bother him. But torture purely for vengeance was utterly different, and an insult to even associate it with her.*

He loved her, so why wasn't he with her? Dan decided then he was done with all of it. He was going to retire from active duty and be with her where he belonged. He brought his attention back to Aco. He wouldn't risk Aco getting away to hurt one more person, and if he had it his way, Aco would be the last time he ever had to kill.

As if signifying the finality of his decision, he plunged the Ka-bar into the man's heart. Aco immediately looked up at Dan with shock, then with the most hateful look Dan had ever seen, followed by a curse he couldn't finish before dying.

Dan rose, crouching on his feet as the situation hit him, along with... the smell of what came out of Aco's corpse. His mind no longer on the struggle between life and death; he felt the breeze cooling his sweat, neither of which he had noticed until now. He couldn't believe he had survived, and the girls were safe, yet there was excitement over his decision and hope for the future with Sonya. *But it couldn't really be over, could it?* Just to be sure, he asked for a sitrep from Paul. Receiving the all-clear, he looked down, surprised at his bleeding arm. He looked down at his chest armor and saw it was covered with blood. It was mangled by a few rounds he could not recall but evident given the rounds embedded in his body armor, not helping his sore ribs. However, considering Kevlar alone without a plate was not supposed to protect you from multiple high caliber shots, he knew someone had been watching over him.

He ripped his cut sleeve off and quickly cleaned and wrapped it with the bandage in his med kit. Going against standard procedure, he took his

Kevlar vest off because he didn't want the girls seeing the blood or the holes. He knew he would hurt when the adrenaline wore off, but this was not his first rodeo. Walking around to the back of the truck, he saw all the girls were accounted for and tried to calm and assure them they were safe. He told them to wait there, and he would be right back. He hurriedly pulled the dead driver out of the truck cab and stopped the engine of the truck, bringing an eerie silence after so much noise.

Walking back to the truck's rear, he smiled at the girls and told them his name was Dan. Paul came on the radio.

"I don't know how… you did it!? It was like you couldn't be touched."

"Ha, couldn't be touched? I have some cuts, bruises, and broken ribs that would disagree." Dan chuckled until he was reminded of his sore ribs.

"We will be at your position in one minute." said Paul over the radio, "we had to take care of a few loose ends."

"Thanks, buddy. Hey, uh, this was my last one, I've decided it's time for me to be present for Sonya."

There was silence as Paul tried to comprehend the news, but truthfully, he wasn't surprised.

"Wow, you couldn't have waited to tell me this in person. I mean, I'm not really surprised. I know how much Sonya means to you and... I wish you, well, brother."

Dan smiled at the finality in Paul's voice.

"Ah, come on, it's not like you'll never see me again, I haven't hit 20 years yet. They'll just keep me stateside training the next generation, maybe you and your family can come to Arizona and meet Sonya."

"All right man, I'd like to meet this Sonya; the only woman that could ever tame the Avenging Angel. Take it easy, I'll be right there."

Paul sounded happy, which made Dan happy. Paul smiled. He guessed his prayer had been answered. He could only hope things between Dan and Sonya went the way Dan hoped.

*

Laying there in the Afghani dirt, Dan recalled the last few moments in slow motion. He heard the door squeak open behind him, turned, at the same time, he heard Paul shout, "NOOOO!" Followed by a stream of profanity over the radio. With the speed of an old West gunslinger, his sidearm was in his hand. But he was not prepared to see a skinny boy no older than 12 with a pistol shouting "Abbi rajulun azeem (my dad is a great man)" Dan tried to pull the trigger, but for some reason, his finger wouldn't work. The boy shot three times, the first two hitting him in the stomach, and the third grazing his thigh before a shot from somewhere to his side took the boy's life. If he had not seen it happen, he wouldn't have thought he had been shot. He hardly felt anything, just a warm feeling, but looking down at his stomach, he knew what had happened, he was a dead man.

He smiled to himself, remembering the promise he would serve God in whatever way he was asked... He thought that meant as a soldier at peace settling down with Sonya... *No! He had to get through this, surely, he couldn't die? Not yet, his mission couldn't be done, and he was going to marry Sonya someday.*

His thoughts were forced back to the current situation when he felt hands gripping him, placing him on a stretcher preparing the chopper.

"Paul, where you at?" Dan asked

From his side, he heard.

"I'm here, Campbell, the chopper, will be here in 20. Don't worry, we'll get you patched up."

Paul wanted to talk about anything that would get Dan's mind off the present situation. But Dan knew what he was doing because he had done it with dying men countless times himself.

Dan couldn't dismiss the sense of irony he felt. "Ha… I always said you should have been an actor or a lawyer with how good you are at lying, Paul…" The weak smile left his face to be replaced by seriousness. "The unit is yours, don't let the work stop here; we still got a lot more people to save. You know it's a shame I'm not a Viking. Dying in combat holding my weapon… The girls, are they safe?"

Just then, Dan and Paul felt a few drops of water and smelled the sweet scent of desert rain.

"Hey, don't talk like that, we're going to get you out of here, and you saved them all! I have never seen anything like it… it was the most incredible thing I've ever seen! I don't think anyone else could have done what you just did. When you retire, you should work in Hollywood and tell them that line, I'm not going to kill. --"

Dan managed to open an eye and look at his friend, "Paul, I'm not afraid to die. I know where I'm going, and I will be ok. Continue, my work, and remember you have two letters to deliver."

"No, don't talk like that man, the chopper's almost here, and you can talk to your mom and Sonya in person."

This time Dan opened both eyes and tried to point at Paul. He was only able to whisper. "I'm giving you an order! The unit's yours, carry on… Deliver my letters! Tell my mom I love her… and" his hand fell, and he could no longer hold his eyes open. "And… tell Sonya… I'll always…" Those were the last words he spoke in life.

Dan slipped in and out of consciousness, but wasn't able to talk. He knew it had started raining, he was in a chopper and heard commotion surrounding him and could feel people working on his body.

Thoughts of parents, family, and the beautiful childhood he'd had swarmed his mind. *He didn't know why, but he had always loved movies and reading about knights. They instilled the idea that a man was supposed to protect and serve women at all costs. Then one day, he met Sonya Young. There was no way he couldn't have fallen in love with her. It was like he had always known her. Thoughts returned to the night; he told her of his feelings and hopes for a future with her. That was when she first told him of the abuse from her past, and she wouldn't let him go through that with her.* Dan had never been one to give up, and he never would give up on Sonya.

That night many years ago, brought Dan to where he was today. He went home that night and announced he was quitting football, to the shock of all of his coaches and family, to focus on the essential things in life. That was when his road to Annapolis began. He attended for two years, served a mission for his church, returned, became an officer, and soon after, a Navy

Seal. But in front of, behind, and around every decision and memory, was Sonya and her beautiful face. She was the most beautiful woman on earth. If she had flaws, he did not see them. She was a part of him. Her beautiful soul and kindness encircled his heart. Perhaps he couldn't marry her now, but she was his best friend and a part of his family. He couldn't imagine loving someone else, and he was a patient man.

He was momentarily pulled back to the present. The worry and emotion in the voices of his men and medics was unmistakable. He was starting to feel more pain now, as the adrenaline wore off. His guts felt like they were on fire, yet he still felt at peace because he knew where he was going.

Then he heard, "he's gone," he tried to speak but couldn't get words out. *What? no, I'm not, I'm…*

*

Paul couldn't believe it. His best friend had done the impossible only to be killed by a 12-year-old boy. Right now, the fact he had shot the boy wasn't bothering him, but the fact he had just watched his friend's dreams vanish in a minute devastated him. He closed his eyes; it was all he could do not to curse God. *I thought you were a loving God. I thought you would've helped him. Surely he deserved love? I'm done asking you for help! You don't care. If you cared, you would've let Dan have his chance at love and happiness.*

Paul couldn't go on. It would take a lot for him to ever trust God again if

he even existed at all. It would take more than he could imagine right now

to ever believe again.

CHAPTER 2
PEACE AND REST?

Dan's eyes popped open. He awoke saying "still here!" and then laughed

realizing, he must've been having a nightmare. It was so bright out, he must

have fallen asleep in the field. He learned not to question anything upon

first waking up anymore. In this line of work, he was never in the same

place very long.

Sitting up, he had no idea where he was. It was a valley with mountains on

all sides and a field full of wildflowers with one shade tree in the middle. It

smelled nothing like Afghanistan and certainly didn't look like it either. The

flowers were all colors and had a refreshing clean smell. Beyond not looking

like Afghanistan, the surroundings looked like no place he had ever seen or

imagined. He looked down and saw he was dressed in white. It was as

bright as mid day, but he couldn't see the sun. Was he having a dream while

in a dream? He once had a dream where he died, it was a bit terrifying. As he looked around, he hoped Sonya would be with him. He always had interesting dreams. Sometimes, it was uncanny how they would predict things. He had found more than one person, who needed his assistance thanks to a dream.

A sidewalk traveled from the lone shade tree to a gate, which in turn led to something best described as a parking lot. *What a strange dream,* he thought. As Dan stood up, he was surprised to find he felt no aches or pains in his body. He couldn't remember the last time nothing hurt; this had to be a dream. Trying to get his bearings in this new place, he looked around. As he looked toward the parking lot, he heard footsteps and voices from the direction of the tree. He immediately reached for a weapon and was shocked to find himself unarmed, which proved this had to be a dream. Dan decided his safest bet was to charge the attackers and catch them off guard. He turned and saw a group of men walking towards him in the same attire as his. Letting his guard down, he observed the group and walked to meet them. Drawing closer, the men seemed familiar. He was trying to place where he knew them from, when suddenly it all became clear.

These weren't just any men. These were his grandfathers, and uncles some he had only known through pictures and stories. Seeing his ancestors made Dan realize he was not dreaming and a new realization hit. He remembered the pain from his dream, and somehow, he woke up without hurting! He always woke up with at least sore knees, and that was on a good day. No, he

hadn't been dreaming about being shot; he really had been. He was dead.

The group of his grandfathers and uncles stood silently, smiling at him. Dan

stood there silent as well until finally cracking an unsure smile and thinking.

It wasn't a dream. I really did die.

"I uh… I always wondered what dying would feel like, I guess I

know now. It's so peaceful and restful. I can't remember the last time I felt

like this. I thought it would have been a bigger transition. I mean, where's

the light they tell you not to go to? It's like I just poofed here. One second

I'm on a battlefield, and the ne- -." The sudden memory of his decision to

be done with military life to settle down with Sonya struck him hard and

left him feeling drained.

He fell to his knees as he told the men,

"I was done, I was going to be with Sonya."

The men came forward, pulling him up and embracing him. He doubted he

would have known some of them when he was still alive, but now

somehow, he remembered them all. Next from the tree came his

grandmothers and aunts. They all hugged and kissed his cheek or forehead,

both those he had known in life and those he hadn't. The joy he felt was

indescribable!

From the other side of the tree across the valley's whole width, people

continued to appear. They all cheered and acted as though they knew him.

He thought, *perhaps these are my ancestors? But why would they know me?* He was

one of the millions of their descendants. Then suddenly, all the cheering

stopped, leaving a complete silence. Dan heard a gate closing behind him,

followed by footsteps coming towards him. Dan froze in place, the way

everyone stopped and him being dead. *Was he about to meet… HIM?* He felt

a hand on his shoulder, and everything stopped as he slowly turned around.

He tried to prepare himself for who he was about to see. The man in front

of him didn't look as Dan imagined HE would have looked like. The man

had dishwater blonde hair, light blue eyes, and looked like a regular person.

His smile and demeanor reminded Dan of a stereotypical California surfer

dude. He had broad shoulders and the build of a man who worked hard

every day farming or ranching. The man gave a warm smile while shaking

his head.

"No, I'm not him, but I do work for him. My name is Abel, and

I've been expecting you for a while now."

Dan's body jolted, and his eyes grew large. "Abel? … Wait… Abel, as in the

son of Adam and Eve, the one who Cain slew?"

A look of sadness crossed his face.

"Yes, that's me…"

Dan cringed and broke an apology into the pause.

"I'm sorry that's probably a hard subject. I'm uh, I'm sorry for how you died…"

Abel looked up a sad smile on his face.

"It's not me that should be pitied, but rather my brother Cain. He made his choice and must pay for it. But enough about me. I'm sure you realized by now you are dead, but that doesn't mean your work is done."

Dan's breath caught in his throat when he heard that his work wasn't done. *Did that mean he could still go back?*

"I oversee a program called Rectify, and you have a choice. You can either continue with your family to the other side of the tree and be done with your earthly work, or you can work for a higher cause, Rectify. This work won't be easy, but you will have the ability to change events from the past and right injustices. Particularly, wrongs done against and affecting women, not always just women, but you will serve the innocent in all cases."

Dan had been looking off to the side at the people continuing to appear and was quite sure he would go with them since he was dead. Those thoughts ended immediately upon hearing offenses against women, his head turned directly towards Abel.

"Yes! Whatever it is, yes!" Then his eyes widened. "Does that mean I'll be able to stop—"

Abel raised his hand. "We will talk about that tomorrow, and don't worry, your family is not saddened by your choice they knew you would accept when I said those words, everyone that knows you, knew you would accept. Before we talk, you have more people to meet, and then you have your funeral and burial to attend. First," pointing to his left "these are the families of all the victims you saved throughout your life."

Looking to the left, Dan saw countless people smiling at him with tears in their eyes. They walked towards him, surrounding him, thanking him for all his efforts on their behalf and their loved ones. He was returning their smiles and receiving their hugs and handshakes, trying not to get emotional himself. Then the next faces stopped him. Collapsing to his knees, he could hardly swallow. These were the faces he saw every day, both on his wall and in his mind. They were the ones he had been unable to save or locate but promised every day he would do his best. Every time he made that promise, he felt the guilt of not finding all of them. He frequently woke from nightmares of searching for these women only to wake in a sweat, never finding them, or being too late. Kneeling before them, he realized he had failed them. Tears welled in his eyes, as he begged for their forgiveness. He had tried his best. Astonishment filled Dan, when they all forgave him.

They had watched him never give up and were most grateful for the peace he brought their families. When everyone else gave up, Dan Campbell continued until he found them, their remains, or stopped the perpetrators. They knew things that no one else knew because they watched him. They knew about his nightmares and his inner-most feelings he had never revealed.

When not on-call or standby, his time was spent searching jungles and waste places for the missing or tracking down those who took them. Many men died on these personal trips, most had bounties on their heads, but Dan never collected. The peace of mind in knowing he had done his all, was reward enough. However, despite all his efforts, he rarely found any of the women or children he searched for. He was usually too late.

As suddenly as they had appeared, they were gone. All thoughts of disappointment and feelings of failure at not finding these women and children had mostly vanished. Beyond the feelings of peace and not having physical pain, he felt most refreshed by knowing they were grateful for his efforts. He continued to look where those people had been, his face full of thought, his mouth moving as he thought to himself.

Abel walked up from behind and stood next to him, making his presence known but not pulling Dan from his contemplations until he was ready. Turning to his left to speak to Abel, Dan felt unable to convey his feelings; there were so many thoughts in his mind.

Abel smiled. "Time passes much differently here. All your efforts on Earth seemed long and difficult to you, but here, they were only a moment. The pain at not being able to find your charges was a tiny fraction of what…" Pointing upward, "…He feels, but you can help him and perhaps find more peace for yourself. There are many more than these few who have been hoping for someone like you. All who have ever been severely wronged or had their blood spilled innocently have been waiting for you. Soon you will not be known as Dan Campbell: The Avenging Angel, but Rectify, because you are the one who will rectify the wrongs done to the innocent. Now look to your right, then it's time for you to get to your funeral. I will explain more when you return."

What's so special about me? Dan thought to himself as he turned.

Looking to his right, he saw his family members waving goodbye to him, he waved back. Following Abel's finger, his eyes were directed back towards the tree. In seemingly endless ranks stood all his ancestors who had served in a military role wearing their uniforms. Looking down, he saw he was wearing his white Lieutenant Commander uniform. He had always

41

preferred his Navy dress whites. He may have been a Major in the Army,

but he was still listed as a Lieutenant Commander in the Navy due to

secrecy.

He looked back at his uniformed ancestors in their ranks and even

recognized a few men at the front he had served with. His uncle, who was

awarded the Silver Star with an Oak Leaf Cluster in Vietnam, stood at the

men's side in his Air Force Colonel's uniform. He saw other uncles and

great uncles saluting in their World War II uniforms. He saw a grandfather

and a few others in World War I uniforms; there were men in Union and

Confederate uniforms, American Revolutionary soldiers, and British

redcoats standing side-by-side saluting. Farther back in the ranks, he saw

men wearing kilts, and suits of armor, all gave many different types of

salutes. For some, it was a fist on their chest. Instead of helmets, some wore

crowns. He guessed these were his royal ancestors, he was connected to

European royalty many generations ago. Beyond the royalty were soldiers

from various kingdoms and periods of history.

Dan was filled with a sense of awe he had never felt before. *Who was he to*

have kings and warriors of the past saluting him? When his uncle ended the

salute, the others did as well. Just as quickly as they had appeared, all left

except for his Uncle Dale. Uncle Dale was one of his personal heroes and

one of the most decorated combat pilots of the Vietnam war. What really made him great was that he never bragged. Dan had no idea how decorated Dale was or genuinely heroic he had been until he passed away, and heard Dale's life story. Dan couldn't hide his beaming smile as his uncle walked up and gave him a hug. Pulling away from the hug, Dale looked him up and down.

"You know I almost joined the Navy, but the recruiter was out to lunch, so the Army Air Corps recruiter snagged me. I have to admit those dress whites do look good, maybe not as good as my Air Force uniform, but way better than an Army dress uniform." They both shared a laugh.

"OK, Dan, you ready to go? Everyone's waiting for you down there. Since I'm also buried in Arlington, I get to go with you. But first, we will stop at your service back home."

Dan's mind was struggling to comprehend all he had just experienced. He had died a short time ago and now minutes or hours later was going to his funeral, which had to have been at least a week or two from when he was killed. His mind was struggling to keep up. Dan decided to go along for the ride and stop wondering about the time stuff.

Dale took Dan by the arm as they walked to the gate, which opened by itself. The first step was through the gate, the next was into the chapel back home, where he had gone to church as a young man. They stood in the back with many of his family members and old friends who were also deceased. At every funeral Dan had ever been to, he always wished he could see and know if there were deceased family members in attendance. A few times, he almost thought he could feel them, one of which was his uncle's funeral. He was pleased to find his suspicions were correct. Some stood in the back, others in the aisles, some sat next to living family members comforting them, though they could not be seen or physically felt. He walked to the front, looking at all there; his throat growing thick. He could feel his eyes well with tears as he saw his parents and family cry. The tears flowed as he saw his deceased grandparents sitting with them.

He was pleased to see Sonya sitting in front with his family, where he had always felt she belonged. He sat down beside her as he looked at her, a sorrow grew which he had never felt before. "What did I do? Why wasn't I there for you?" he said aloud. *Perhaps my attention and dedication to her was more of a disservice than a service? But no, no one could love her like I could.* He felt sorry for how long she would be alone waiting to see him again. Shaking his head, he stood up. He didn't like these thoughts and had no idea where they were coming from.

Walking up to where the officiators and speakers sat, he took a seat looking at the faces of family, friends, and comrades, even Paul and most of his men were there. Tears filled his eyes as he looked at his mother, sister, nieces, and Sonya. He heard some of the life story and barely noticed the sermon. He sat in silence as the chapel emptied. His uncle sat down beside him, placing a hand on his shoulder.

"Dan, it will be alright, you'll see. Now, do you want to stay here or shall we get to Arlington for your burial?"

Dan's head shot up, startled from his ponderings, and looked to his uncle in puzzlement.

"Surely, we have time! It's a long way from Arizona to Virginia."

Laughing, Dale replied, "Ha time…" shaking his head. "Time hardly matters now, and there's no reason to wait; we have work to do, let's go and it will be time."

As they exited, the chapel they were met with a scene far different from an Arizona fall. Instead of an early October with trees covered in green leaves and the smell of warm dry air, he was instead met with trees sparsely dressed in red leaves, some on their branches, some at their base. The air was crisp, wet, and smelled of damp grass. He looked around at thousands of headstones, as a funeral hearse pulled up next to a caisson pulled by horses, and an honor guard transferred the casket. Their precision and exactness nearly brought tears to his eyes. This honor guard indeed displayed honor, and the military band played with perfect military precision.

Most of his family and friends were gathered. He guessed his parents were already at the burial site because of the long walk. The band began beating a cadence. Along with an escort, the march to the burial site launched, the soldiers walking in perfect unison. Behind the caisson followed family and friends, both the living and the dead. As they marched, Dan saw the spirits of soldiers lining both sides of the road, standing at full attention. He started to ask his uncle about them, but Dale already knew his question.

"Those lining the road are the Eternal Sentinels of Arlington. Anyone who has ever been an honor guard at Arlington is asked if they would like to continue their duty after death and most accept. When it comes to The Old Guard, they usually request it. Those who were members of the Tomb guard carry their duty and dedication with them. They continue their watch until they are no longer needed, you should go meet them someday."

Dan wondered why they would still need to carry their duty on after death, what could possibly be the need now?

No more was said. Continuing the procession, Dan couldn't help but look into the unfaltering gaze of each silent and unmoving sentinel.

Finally, the honor guard and the caisson stopped at their destination, which was Dan's final destination, as far as his physical body was concerned. He watched as his casket was removed from the caisson and placed over his plot. Words and dedications were said, but Dan barely noticed any of those. He was walking among his parents, siblings, nieces, nephews, and friends. How he wished he would have spent more time with each of them in life. He halted and quickly moved on when he saw Sonya sitting next to his mother and father, all three in tears. He was not ready for those feelings yet. Perhaps if he could have done it all over again, he would've done things differently, but that wasn't possible now. He was touched to see so many friends he had grown up with in school and church. He supposed someday he would have the opportunity to tell them how much it meant to see them there. Then he looked over and saw Paul and so many he had served with throughout his military career.

Coming back to stand by his uncle, he was gently nudged in the ribs and directed to look around. Doing so, he was filled with a feeling beyond description. Standing in front of almost every headstone in Arlington was the hero buried there, looking straight at him. *Indeed, Arlington is one of the most sacred places in the United States*; he thought to himself as he felt tears stream down his cheeks. The ceremonies and proceedings began, but Dan's thoughts were somewhere else; it all seemed so physical. How could he be dead? His thoughts ventured to his family members, feeling their sorrow;

his thoughts continued in this manner until the sound of rifles firing broke him out of his reverie.

He watched a silent specter, as most of his military comrades and old friends filtered away, leaving only his family, Paul Gutierrez, and some senator. Apparently, one of the girls Dan had rescued caught his first and last name, and someone informed this senator. He went to Dan's family, telling them more than he should have about Dan's work, assuring them he would do his best to see that Dan got the medal of honor. The number of things he knew made Dan wonder if this senator had something to do with his last mission. It seemed most senators never got the whole top-secret thing...

He and his uncle both looked at each other. "He must be up for re-election," Dan said, rolling his eyes as the senator and his entourage left.

His uncle laughed. "I don't know but, why don't you go over there and let your mom know you're here."

"How do I do that?"

His uncle looked at him, "I guess it depends on how much faith you have. You've always had a lot of faith, why should it work any differently when you're dead?"

Dan walked over to his mother, who was still sitting in a chair overlooking his casket. He shed a few tears seeing his mother's sorrow. He was usually strong until he saw a woman he cared about crying. He thought to himself, *I know I can make her feel that I'm here.* Mustering up all his love for her, he knelt down in front of her. With her hands atop the flag in her lap, he put his hand over hers.

He didn't feel her physically as he would've when he was alive but felt her at a deeper level. He knew she had sensed him when she lifted her face. She seemed to be looking straight at him, and amidst tears, she managed a smile and spoke.

"He's here. I can feel him!" All who remained looked to where she was looking. "I can't see you, Dan, but I know you're here, and I know you'll always be watching over us. I love you and know I will see you again someday." The others also told him they loved him, mostly for his mother's sake. After they finished, his mother again spoke. "Dan, as much as I want you to stay here, I know you have more to do, and I will not keep you from your work."

"I love you, Mom!" His mother was always about duty, and love caused another tear to fall as he thought about her incredible role in his life. His father and one brother served in the Navy, which influenced his decision to join the Navy. They were not the ones who instilled his dedication to duty. His mother was one of the most significant reasons he cared so much about duty and helping people. However, at this moment, if given a chance to do it all over again, he would not have rushed off to the military. He would have spent more time with his parents to learn more about them. But then the only way he wouldn't have joined the military after 9/11 was if he was physically unable. With a final smile at his sweet mother, he closed his eyes, let go, and stood up.

He walked to each person, touching each in turn. Some felt it and some didn't. Looking back towards his casket, he saw Sonya. She was often able to keep her emotions in check, but now she was touching the coffin unable to control her tears. He saw Paul standing nervously off to the side with the two letters in his hands, obviously unsure of what to do next. It was strange to see Paul so vulnerable and frightened. This man who had stared death in the face countless times now looked as though delivering a few letters was the most dangerous thing in the world. Dan walked over to Paul, hoping he could do something to help him.

*

Paul was raised Catholic, but quit going when he was a teenager. Sure, sometimes he would go on Easter or at Christmas, at his wife's insistence, but he wouldn't go out of his way to attend church. Paul had been fairly certain there was a God and he answered prayers, but all that changed the day Dan died. Dan had served a mission for his church. He followed their stupid rules, like the whole no alcohol thing, he didn't cuss, and always went to church if he could. As far as Paul knew, Dan had never even had sex, and it wasn't for lack of opportunity. Women threw themselves at Dan all the time.

Paul's wife always joked; she would marry Dan if she ever became single. Paul was sure she was joking, but he had noticed how she and the other women lit up when Dan smiled. He noticed the way women looked at Dan when they attended parties, especially pool or beach parties. *Stupid Navy Seals, just because they are Seals, doesn't mean they have anything a Green Beret doesn't.* Dan always knew how to compliment a woman and make her feel good about herself. Paul never worried because he trusted his wife and everyone knew Dan was faithful to Sonya. Dan thought he was a knight of sorts, and Sonya was his lady love. The men had hired women to try to seduce Dan more than once, and each time, they had Dan's views physically pounded into them.

But obviously, following all the rules did not mean anything to God. Paul was angry at God for allowing this to happen. Dan always said God loved humans as his literal children. If God really loved him, why did he let Dan die instead of letting him have a chance with Sonya. Paul's feelings had softened some in the past week from hearing the sermons, and people talk about Dan's belief

51

in life after death. For Dan's sake, Paul hoped it was true. Dan deserved to have a chance at the love he yearned for and to find peace. His feelings had softened, but it would take a lot to change his mind. Paul stood to the side of Dan's casket, for who knows how long with the two letters in his hand. He was not sure how to approach the intended recipients. Then the strangest thing happened; he half-heard, half-felt something.

"Paul, I'm here, and I'm okay. Now deliver my letters! I'm here, and I always will be."

At that, Paul moved his eyes back and forth as if trying to determine if he genuinely had heard something. Seeing a bird perched on a nearby branch, he convinced himself that was what he heard. Dan patted his shoulder and pushed him on the back, towards the two most important women in his life, causing Paul to jump.

"Campbell, is that you?" He whispered softly, eyes scanning his surroundings but seeing nothing. "Okay, Da-uh Geez... even in death, you're a hard-- I mean pushy." Dan hoped Paul knew how much he appreciated his respect for his beliefs and principles.

"I don't know where you are, Campbell or how you're doing this. But I'm getting there." He walked in the direction of Mrs. Campbell, muttering under his breath...

"Mrs. Campbell, I had the honor of serving with your son, and I was there at the end. He was… IS one of the greatest men I have ever known. You know I cannot tell you much about what we do or did, but you would be very proud of your son! I believe out of all the heroes who have ever existed, he was perhaps the greatest, and he deserved far more medals than he had. You were an ever-present part of his life, and his last thoughts were of you and Sonya…"

*

With Paul well on his way, Dan walked to Sonya's side, putting his hand on her shoulder, she turned to her shoulder. Dan guessed she felt him because a slight smile crossed her lips despite the sadness in her eyes. He stood there, until Paul walked over with a letter stretched out in front of him.

*

"Hi Sonya, my name is Paul."

Sonya smiled. "Oh, you're Paul! Dan talked about you all the time. I'm glad he had you as a friend."

Paul smiled, thrown off by Sonya, interrupting his prepared speech.

"Hmm, I bet he didn't talk about me as much as he talked about you."

She again smiled. "No, I bet he didn't. I'm sorry, Paul, I interrupted you, please continue."

"Thanks Sonya, um I was with Dan… at well the end, and he asked me to deliver letters to his mother and you. He talked about you all the time, about what a wonderful person you are, and pretty much-dedicated everything he ever did to you. His last words were of you. The world lost a great man…" Paul's voice cracked, almost betraying the emotions he was trying to hide.

"Thank you for your time. Also, I know you are here somewhere, Campbell, so see, I delivered your letters. See you soon, brother, we will make you proud." He hesitated like he had more to say, Dan half-hoped, half-feared Paul would tell Sonya he was planning to quit to be with her. If Dan didn't know better, he would've thought he saw a tear forming as Paul turned to hurry away.

"Thank you, Paul, I know he's here next to me," Sonya replied, not noticing he was gone. Her attention became intent on opening and reading the letter.

"My dear Sonya, I hope you never have to read this letter, but if you do, I'm sorry. I don't know how much they were able to tell you, but let me just say, you've been the inspiration of my life. I have done all I can to protect others from the same things you had to endure. I'm sure they've sent all my belongings already, and I want you to keep the knife you gave me. I carried it on every mission and always touched it before going into danger to remind myself of you and your smile. I will always be with you, and I will always love you!"

Sniffing, she closed the letter and held it to her chest. She was pleased the knife meant so much to him. Unfortunately, the knife the had not been recovered.

"I've always loved you too, Dan! I'm sorry I couldn't express it, but I'm glad you knew I did... I will take care of your mother as though she were my own. I guess they needed you on the other side more than we did, so go do whatever it is you must do, and I will see you again someday... You will always be my hero," she said, tears falling from her sad brown eyes!

How Dan wished she could have felt his hug. After standing there next to Sonya for a few more minutes, he looked up and walked back to his uncle. He took a lingering look at his family, sorrowing for the pain they were going through. But smiled, knowing someday they would be together again, and it likely wouldn't seem that long from his perspective. He still wasn't sure what precisely this Rectify program entailed but guessed he was ready to find out. Looking over to his uncle,

"Well, I guess I'm ready, lead out."

Taking two steps, the gate once again appeared with Abel, standing next to the entrance. The gate automatically opened, and his uncle walked through, but a hand on Dan's chest from Abel stopped him.

"No, you have somewhere else to go. I need to teach you about your role as Rectify."

Dale turned around from the other side of the gate, Dan saluted him, with his uncle returning it. They then waved to each other, and he was gone. Dan turned back to Abel.

"OK, Dan, that's enough rest."

"What? I wanted to talk to my Grandpa and Grandma before I started this mission."

Abel took a breath. "Don't worry, you have nothing but time, and they'll understand. Right now, it's time to get busy because you have a lot of work to do. Let's step into my office."

Instantly they were in an office of white from the floor to ceiling. Abel took a seat behind the desk, motioning for Dan to take a seat in front of it. Dan sat without thinking, awed by their sudden transition from place to place.

CHAPTER 3
TIME TO WORK

"How did that just happen? We were outside, I guess, at the waiting place between life and death. Now suddenly, we are here... How?".

Abel smiled and nodded. He was expecting this question.

"We are in a different plane of existence, much of it dealing with your perception. When you're first introduced to things here, you will perceive them as whatever is most understandable to you. Gradually you will recognize things by their true nature. As you gain more control over your thoughts, it will become more natural, and you will find no limit to what you can do. Things you once would have considered impossible will soon seem as natural as your heart beating. The things you once pondered about the universe and its workings will eventually be easily understood, and you will wonder how you didn't know that before."

Dan shrugged his shoulders and tipped his head to the right thinking about Abel's words. It actually made sense. With every subject, you always start with the basics before you can understand the more complicated things. It was like algebra. He struggled with it for a long time until he finally recognized that the lower levels of algebra built up to the higher levels. After he realized how important it was to know the basics of algebra, he could get it.

"Okay, Abel, I guess I will come to understand later. I trust you will teach me the things I need to know, and actually, I look forward to learning the secrets of the universe and having all my questions answered. As to this Rectify program, how will I rectify things for people when I'm dead, and they're dead. Isn't it a bit late for that?

Abel pursed his lips, visibly thinking.

"Hmmm, I will just tell it to you straight. You aren't exactly dead, and you aren't exactly alive right now. You were correct about the place you saw when you first arrived; it was an in-between place. Sometimes, people tell stories where they died and then came back. Well, this is the place they saw, they just don't remember it properly. In your mortal state, things go slow, but here, they are very fast, so when they say they went to the light, it's because their recollection seems slow, but yet it was fast, so the time differentiation…"

Abel noticed that Dan was looking at him like he had no idea what he was talking about, so he decided to simplify it more.

"Let me try that again. Uh um… Look here's the basics: you are still you and always will be, but you will be changed so you can move back and forth between earth and here freely, well mostly, and still retain your body. If you were not a good man, we would not be in this office having this conversation. Throughout the history of the…" Abel paused momentarily as he thought about the next word… "world, there've been very few with the ability, knowledge, and worthiness to fulfill your role.

Dan's ears perked up when he mentioned that there'd been very few qualified for this position.

"There've been others. Like who?" Dan asked with emphasis.

Abel chuckled then straightened up. "Does it matter who they were? There is only one Rectify, and that is you. From the beginning to the end, you have been, are, and always will be, Rectify."

This time it was Dan's turn to laugh, "Thanks for trying to make me feel special, but if I just now died, how could I have been Rectify from the beginning of time? Not even looking at the time problem, how can I be worthy when I've killed so many people? How can I be good enough or worthy to be in this position? Surely not everyone I killed was a disgusting human being or deserving of death."

Abel put his hands on the desk, interlocking his fingers as he thought for a time.

"Did you ever kill someone outside of combat or a mission?

"Well, not exactly..." Dan wasn't sure about some of his personal missions he had gone on.

"I know what you are thinking, and while you were not ordered to go on your personal missions. Did you enjoy killing, when you did it?

"What? Of course, not... Well... OK, here's the problem I didn't necessarily enjoy killing any of them, but I honestly wasn't sad to see them go. I was kind of glad I got to be the one to... bring them to accountability. In the midst of combat, I never really thought of who I was killing; maybe some weren't there by choice, but they knew what was going on. When the shooting started, they should have run if they were truly offended by what they were involved in. At the moment, it was them or me, and when it came to sex trafficking and those who indiscriminately killed innocents, I was glad to remove them from the earth. I will kill an infinite number of sick and wicked people if that's what it takes to save one innocent. But I can truly say, I never really sought out any certain person with the intent to just kill them. But..." Dan bowed his head and placed his hand to his forehead.

"But… NO! What about when I killed Aco? I was happy to do it. We had his whole organization mapped out and didn't need him alive, because we were taking out the entire organization. We had SF teams of all branches taking out the whole infrastructure, but I didn't want him to escape. I basically lied to him and then murdered him, and I was glad to do it, but then his son died as a result. If I hadn't killed his dad and let him live, that boy would still be alive. I didn't have to kill Aco; I probably broke rules of engagement… But," Dan paused. "I hated Aco and imagined killing and torturing him almost every day."

Abel listened to everything Dan said, then at the first opportunity interrupted him.

"Dan, look at me, if you hadn't killed Aco, then he would've escaped at a future point and continued his work; evil organizations can be rebuilt. As far as his boy, his was a case where he was so inundated with propaganda and his father's example that he would've become just like him. Though it's hard to accept, he would have nourished that hatred and unleashed a greater evil on the world than his father could have ever imagined. Perhaps more evil than any on earth has ever committed. You weren't the first person that boy killed. Still, because he had no chance of escaping that indoctrination and was so young, he won't be judged for anything he did, you may have done him a favor."

"You, of course, know God has an enemy, known by many names, you know him as Lucifer. Others know him as Abaddon, Adramalech, Ahpuch, Dagon, Shiva, Fenrir, and many, many more, some names are lost to history. He is always grooming monsters for his work, and not always who you would think. Most wars and human conflict have occurred because of human greed, lust, and other vices, but not all. The longer you are Rectify, the more you will fight Lucifer and his minions. You will come to find most of his monsters are unknown, and he and his followers operate in the shadows. You have unknowingly removed some of his best pawns in your life. You may also find that there is a greater evil out there that you've never imagined., which you will have to fight.

"Besides, you have no need to worry about killing Zaman Aco, because you didn't. Rick Adams did!" Abel said with a smile spreading across his face.

Dan furrowed his eyebrows, blinking in confusion, "What? Who? I've never heard of a Rick Adams..."

Abel smiled. "Don't you remember what you said? It belongs in a book or movie. You said, "I'm not killing you, the Marine who owns this knife is, I'm just the delivery boy."

"That Marine was Rick Adams. He was a man much like you, Marine Recon, but was killed by Aco several years ago when he tried to rescue some women from Aco. Rick was beyond pleased about it, and honestly, I was too. Aco was a wicked man and committed unforgivable atrocities. So, you see, Dan, you are fit to be Rectify, you always have been, and you've always had a knack for reading people, which will definitely come in handy."

Dan sat back in his seat, rubbing his chin, which was the first time he had realized he was clean-shaven. *When did that happen? Wait, I'm ok?*

"Oh man, this is a huge relief, I've always worried about this moment. I'm… I just wasn't sure. Thank you, Abel! But where do I go now?"

"Don't worry, God knows the intent of your heart, and if you enjoyed the killing, you would not be sitting across from me right now. However, to be Rectify, you will still need to kill, but now you will only be able to kill humans who are irredeemable.

Why did he specify humans and not men, passed through Dan's head.

"Any killing blow you inflict on someone who is redeemable will not die but will fall unable to move, and have the opportunity to change their life. You will have the added benefit of knowing the intents others have and knowing you can only kill the ones God allows. Your work will not involve the present; it will almost exclusively deal with wrongs from the past. You will also come to understand why I say humans, and unfortunately, not all women are innocent like your Sonya."

Dan opened his eyes in surprise. Choosing to ignore that Abel just read his mind.

"So, let me get this straight, there's no way I can kill an innocent person?"

Abel's nod to the affirmative filled him with excitement to start the program. Dan was now standing and beginning to pace, which was something he did when excited and planning.

"Alright, so let's get this started. Whoa! I can stop Hitler, Stalin, Mao, and all the evil people who have ever lived." The more he talked, the more he thought, and the louder his voice grew. "Wait, that means I can fix everything in history, I can save William Wallace, I can stop World War II, really every war there ever was and… I can stop--

Abel sprang to his feet. "Whoa, whoa, whoa… hold on! Don't get ahead of yourself. It's not that simple. Remember, there are rules. First, remember not all men you consider evil did it because of the devil. You can't just go around fighting anyone you choose. Yes, your work will be in the past, but it will be the present for everyone else when you are there."

"You must always remember people are free to make choices; we cannot take that away. There are many bad things we must not stop because they lead to other events which, horrific, resulted in good things. You can't save any martyr who died for a good cause because their blood made their words and life more powerful."

"Your primary work will be among the voiceless, the simple, the poor, the meek, basically anyone that's in a bad situation not of their doing. You will help them in ways they cannot help themselves. Your actions will have slight effects on the world. You may find that once your work is done, individuals' names will change. You will still know them, but their names may be different; in fact, your name could change."

Dan was listening to everything but was so overwhelmed he was having trouble comprehending. Then the full scope of what he was doing hit him, causing him to stop mid-pace and turn to look at Abel, his mouth hanging open, blinking.

"Whoa, that's heavy, Doc! So, you're telling me that time travel is possible? I will be time traveling, and you or whoever," Dan directed his thumb up above them, "are just fine with me changing things, and oh, my name could change?"

Abel looked back, a smile crossing his face.

"Great Scott Marty, Yes!"

Dan looked at Abel, a confused look on his face. Abel chuckled. "Hey, I may be dead, but I'm not that dead. I see movies, and if your name does change, you won't know. As to the time stuff, let's just say, think of all time as present but not in the present."

Dan was silently trying to grasp time travel and failing.

"Just leave the time stuff to us," Abel said, smiling. "Mortals never get it right and always leave plot holes when they try to figure it out."

"Now, back to things easier to understand. Do you accept everything I've told you? I already know your next question. The answer is yes; at some point, when you've completed your work, you can help Sonya. But remember, this won't be easy, it will take a great deal of love, and it may not go exactly the way you want."

Dan became serious. "Abel, I don't care how hard it is, and I don't even care if it doesn't go the way I hope. I love her and want her to be happy! I made a promise to God when I was overlooking that compound. When I said I would serve God, I meant it, and by the feeling I had, I know He listened, so I am here to do whatever he asks."

A huge smile crossed Abel's face.

"You pass the test. We were hoping you would remember your

deal. Now we are really ready to begin."

As he finished speaking, the wall of the office vanished, replaced by a giant movie screen.

Dan turned his chair to the screen and started to speak but was cut off by Abel.

"I know what you're thinking, and yes, this will be a presentation of everything you're ready to see."

Dan did a double-take between the screen and Abel.

"Wait, what do you mean by ready to see?"

"Dan, it's hard to explain, because you chose to be here, you can't see everything as you are still in a type of limbo between life and death. Just trust me when I say, you don't want to see everything yet."

Dan had always hoped when he died, there would be a presentation of some sort, giving an overview of everything. Even with his initial disappointment of not seeing everything, this video still went beyond anything he had ever imagined; it showed him and everyone. He understood and felt in his heart that he wasn't only here for revenge but also to fix things. He was going to deliver justice and mercy where needed. He would be an instrument in God's hands. It was amazing how quick the video was. Time really was different now. He also recognized that he was

gaining much more use of his brain, so he understood it all quickly. In fact,

looking back, it felt more like he was in the video than watching it.

The screen disappeared, replaced by the wall. Dan turned back to Abel.

"Wow, that was better than I ever imagined. After seeing all that

and all the people, I'm glad I couldn't feel what they felt… How did He do

it?" Dan asked, looking upwards.

"No one else can comprehend it. The only answer I can give you is

pure love. Love beyond what anyone else is capable." Abel said, tears

streaming down his face. He paused a moment to gather his composure.

"Now, let's get you ready for your first mission."

Dan swallowed hard at the idea that he was going to start his first mission

already.

"Are you sure I'm ready? I don't know anything about this." Dan

stammered. "What if I have to speak another language? What if I need

something when I get there?"

Without explanation or warning, Abel began speaking in what sounded like

an Asian language. Dan stared at him perplexed, he didn't know the

language. But it didn't stop Abel from continuing to speak until finally, he made an exasperated noise.

"How have you not figured out what I'm saying!?" Abel asked in annoyance.

Dan raised his eyebrows, pointing at himself, "Why are you mad at me!? You're the one speaking some language I don't know and looking at me like I'm supposed to know what I'm hearing!"

Abel slapped himself on the forehead. "That explains it. You are hearing, but you are not listening. OK, listen to me again, but this time open your mind and listen as though you know you can understand it."

"If you say so, I'll go ahead and listen." Dan rolled his eyes

Abel started speaking again in the same language, but this time, Dan focused less on the sound and more on the intent behind it. At first, it was incomprehensible, but he listened, imagining that he understood it, and continued listening to whatever Abel was saying.

"… It requires faith. All you have to do is listen, and you will understand whatever language you are hearing- -"

"Hey! I understand you!" Dan exclaimed. "But what language is that?"

"Now that you know how to understand, you don't need to know

69

the language because you will be able to understand any spoken or written

language. It will still sound and look like whatever language is most

comfortable for you, but you will understand all languages. At the deepest

level, all languages are the same; it's only the mortal mind's limitations

keeping people from understanding the feelings, intents, and words of other

people. But if you must know, it was an ancient dialect used in Japan, and I

doubt anyone living now would be able to understand. But in the case of

your work, you will understand what they say to you, and they will hear the

words you speak in their language."

Dan smiled. "That makes sense. I really don't think Japanese

people would understand my English, French, Dutch, Arabic, or my limited

Russian and Farsi. So, the language is taken care of, but what about

equipment and how I get in and out?"

"You will enter wearing the clothes expected of someone of your

needed station. But as the need arises, you can change your garments to

appear as whatever you might choose. You will have the ability to change

items to what you need, though I warn you this will take some time to

figure out. Getting you in and out will be simple; we will just drop you near

the place you need to be. Just think where you want to go, and that's where

you'll be. You will know when the mission is over and when you can start

your next task. Here is a list of all those you will be helping," he said, pointing to the desk.

Dan understood everything Abel said, and it all made sense. *Besides just a few missions and he could help Sonya.* Dan was smiling until he looked to where Abel was pointing. His face dropped; he looked at the list, then back to Abel twice, evidently shocked at what he saw. Indeed it was a list, but it looked about as thick as his fist.

"How many pages is that list?" Dan asked flatly.

"Oh, only about 500 give or take," Abel said, opening a drawer of the desk, taking out 3 more stacks of paper about the same size, stacking them on the pages already there. "So, I guess... oh, I guess it's about 2000 pages. But..." he looked into Dan's eyes and quickly added, "Not to worry, there are only about three or four names per page."

"8000, names!? So essentially, I have six to eight thousand missions to complete before I finish this program!? Everyone I care about will be dead before even I finish 500 of these missions." Dan said a touch of anger in his voice

"Calm down, calm down! I forget how focused we are on time as mortals. It may sound like a long time to you, but time moves differently here than it does back there. Besides, most of your work will be occurring in history before your lifetime, so the time they take won't even affect the people you know. If you're doing it for the right reasons, you won't even notice the time. Besides, some of the missions will take you only a few minutes or hours. However, we are taking you out of the frying pan for your first mission and throwing you into the fire. Usually, the best way to learn is to experience it, and it's not like you can really die, well... don't worry, you'll be just fine."

"Wow, thanks, Abel... That makes it all so much better." Dan said in his driest, most monotone voice. "How am I supposed to know who I help next? Am I supposed to come back here after each mission to get a new one?"

"No, that would be ridiculous! You will memorize them." Abel said

"Memorize it? You gotta be kidding me! It would take me more several weeks to read all that, much less memorize it!" Dan said, almost at a yell.

"Keep your voice down! Don't you realize where you are? And remember, you volunteered for this." Abel said, pointing his finger at Dan's chest. "Surely by now, you've figured out that you have more use of your brain than you used to. So, you can read and remember everything much faster. Also, this is the perfect time to teach you about one of your most important abilities.

Abel got up from his seat and pulled the chair out, indicating for Dan to sit down.

"Dan, what do you see in front of you on the desk?"

A forlorn voice replied, "Four stacks of paper that you want me to read and memorize, page by page.".

"Yes, you see stacks of paper, but what would be a faster and easier way to read all these names instead of page by page?"

Dan thought for a moment. "Probably a computer, tablet, or something so I can scroll through and quickly turn pages, maybe an electronic reader?"

"Yes, great idea! Now I want you to put your hand on one of the stacks and think what you want those pages to become to help read the list faster."

Dan placed his hand on the stack and thought for a moment. But nothing happened, this time he closed his eyes and thought of a computer. Suddenly his hand dropped, landing on a keyboard. Opening his eyes, a desktop computer was in front of him. The keyboard was slightly dingy. It was the old family Tandy 1000.

"Ha, that's the computer we had when I was a kid, but why is it the computer that showed up? There are certainly faster ways of reading this list."

"It became the first thing you thought of, evidently in your mind when you think of a computer this is the first thing you think of. This skill takes some time to get used to. Dan, I want you to try again. This time when you have your hand on the computer, picture what you want it to turn into, keep your eyes open, and think of the most advanced computer you can think of."

He tried again, picturing the most advanced computer he could imagine. This time it was the computer from Star Trek TNG that appeared. Dan couldn't help but laugh out loud. He recalled how Data would sit at the computer and read entire books in seconds. As he thought all these things, he watched the computer change to laptop size. Because the computer on Star Trek was gigantic. He didn't need one that big.

"Whoa, it worked, I think. Let me test it. Ha, this probably won't work, but let's see. Computer, who am I?"

"You are Rectify, a.k.a. Dan Campbell, a.k.a. The Avenging Angel, other titles are withheld at this time." The computer said in a voice like Sonya's.

Dan stared at the computer for a moment.

"Wow, this is amazing! But um… what does it mean other titles are withheld at this time?"

"You will learn those titles in due time," Abel answered, casually brushing it aside.

Dan sighed. "Of course, I die, and I still need a security clearance. Since I'm going to be here a while memorizing this list, I might as well get started." Turning back to the computer, he stated "Display my list."

"Rectify, what speed would you like the list scrolled at?" The computer asked.

"I don't know, I guess the fastest you can go and I can still read and memorize. I was always a fast reader."

"Say activate to begin." The computer again intoned in Sonya's voice.

Dan guessed it was Sonya's voice because that was on his mind. But he knew he wouldn't be able to do anything if it stayed her voice.

"Computer change voice, to Mrs. Winger, my 7th-grade Algebra teacher."

He couldn't stand her, but knew if it was her voice, he couldn't help but hurry so he could turn her off.

Dan stared at a blank computer screen and said activate. Suddenly the pages began to scroll in a blur, and within 30 seconds, the computer chimed list complete.

Looking at Abel, Dan exclaimed. "What was that!? How am I supposed to memorize something that scrolls so fast?"

"Hmm, I don't know, let me test you. What is first on your list?"

Without thinking, Dan answered. "I will help Kaito and his wife, Hana. As I help them, I have to tell them my name is Yuuto. Kaito is a farmer, and his wife is exceedingly beautiful. She is sister to the lord of the village and…"

Dan sat there, shocked for a few heartbeats, as he realized he had it memorized.

"Wait a minute. Abel, why is there so little information? I hate to be that guy, but come on, this isn't much to go on."

"Good question, as we are changing events, we do not know what will transpire after you rescue Hana, well you don't anyway. Therefore, you will have to use your judgment and insight to best help them while they determine their fate. You are Rectify; you need to be able to learn how to judge these things. If you know too much, you may inadvertently mess things up, which is why we aren't telling you the time period, and you won't be able to know some names because that may cause you to change too much." Abel said matter-of-factly.

"That sounds right. Not easy, but right. I should've known it wouldn't be simple." Dan said, without energy.

"You obviously, know the first name on your list. How about the next names?"

Dan proceeded to list off all the names, which he now had memorized in response to Abel.

"Wow, that's amazing! Wait, do I have 100% use of my brain now?"

"No, but you have enough to be able to do your job, and you obviously have all the skills you need. I would say you are ready to begin." Abel said.

"Begin? But I still have so many questions, I barely know anything about sword fighting or the culture.

Abel replied. "I'm sure you have a lot of questions. Your first mission will take place in Japan but don't bother trying to figure out when or where exactly you are, because it doesn't matter. Probably the less you know, the better, because it will just take away from the mission. Focus on

the mission at hand because most of the time, it will be a place, event, or

person you've never heard of. The best way for you to learn is to do.

Forget yourself and go to work. Do your duty, and we will do the rest."

"Well, then, I guess… guess I'm ready. How do I begin?

"Think to yourself where you want to go, then command it," Abel

said.

Dan was about to leave for the mission, but couldn't hold back the question

he had wanted to ask since he and Abel had first started talking.

"If I'm dead, and I've always been Rectify, why don't I remember

it? Why didn't I know who all those people were, who I assumed were

ancestors when I first met you? I thought when I died, I would remember

everything."

Abel smiled. "Remember when I said you weren't exactly dead and

you weren't exactly alive? If you had gone past that tree when you arrived,

you would have remembered everything, but then we wouldn't be here

talking about your mission as Rectify. However, should you choose, you

can leave here, go past that tree, and you will remember everything, but

your purposes on earth will be done. You can make this decision at any

point, remember up here, we are all about choice, so you will always have that freedom.

Dan smiled, "Hey, there's only one choice for me. See you after the mission, Abel." Dan thought of his first mission and was gone.

*

Abel found himself alone smiling while shaking his head, *That's the Rectify I remember as if there was any doubt what your choice would be. I hope you find your joy, Heaven knows you deserve it.* He felt God's love for Dan and just wished Dan could remember what he had done before but knew he would someday. He opened one of the windows of his mind to watch Dan aware many others were doing the same. They knew what Rectify was going to face and were worried at the toll it would take on him, all who could remember the past were well aware of all he had already sacrificed.

CHAPTER 4
RAINY SEASON

The next thing Dan knew, he was standing in a small grove of trees, during

a torrential downpour surrounded by the smell of damp vegetation. No

water hit his face, thanks to the woven brimmed hat he was wearing, some

sort of hard-bottomed sandals and short pants with a short robe completed

his ensemble. Hardly any protection from the elements that could be felt,

but evidently, things were different in his new condition. Lifting his hand to

his face, he could see water on his skin, but it seemed it didn't soak in or at

least didn't have the adverse effects of being soaked. He thought it was odd

and could think of times when not feeling the elements, as usual, could be a

drawback. Before the thought had finished, he felt the dampness that one

should feel when soaked; with another thought, things changed back to

how they were.

Hey, this is pretty cool, guess it's a perk of being a… Hmm, what am I anyway? A clap of thunder snapped him back to where he was. *Oh well, I'll figure it out later.*

Looking more closely at his clothes, he couldn't say he was excited. *This certainly isn't what I thought I'd be wearing after I died.* It was apparent he was in an Asian country sometime in the past. However, had he not been told he was be going to Japan, he wouldn't have known. He was kind of embarrassed, he had pictured himself in samurai armor, not Daisy Dukes and a robe, needless to say, he wasn't used to wearing shorts. He looked up, letting the rain hit his face, again annoyed that he wasn't wearing a cool mask like they did in the movies.

Taking 10 steps, he emerged from the grove of trees looking all around him. Clouds were so thick they almost seemed to touch the ground. The rain was so heavy that all he could make out was the outline of a distant building about 400 steps away. The air smelled better to him now that he was away from the trees. Grass expanded out in all directions, several puddles on the ground revealed it had been raining for a while. He took another step and felt his foot sink into a mud puddle. These sandals really weren't doing much to protect his feet and definitely weren't comfortable to walk in. Maybe he didn't feel the usual effects of the elements, but foot care was so ingrained in him he couldn't shake off the offense. He wished he could do something about the footwear then remembered his ability to transform objects.

He went down to his knee, placing his hand on one of the sandals, closed his eyes, focused his mind on comfortable boots that would actually protect his feet. Nothing happened, then the thought came to his mind how there would be a problem if people saw him wearing modern boots. This time he took the sandals off and held them in his hand; thought of his Bates boots, which were his favorite. They are basically combat boots with the comfort of an athletic shoe that keeps the weather and moisture out. This time, he added the addition that they should appear as the sandals to all but him. Suddenly, the sandals transformed into the very boots he was thinking of, down to the scuff on the side. He held them over the puddle he had been standing in. The reflection showed sandals and the face of a Japanese man he had never seen before.

"Is that me?" he asked aloud, then shook his head and again said aloud, "I am Rectify," instead, he heard Japanese. *Must be what it sounds like in Japanese,* he thought, then remembered he was supposed to be Yuuto.

After he had said Rectify, the sandals appeared as the boots, and his face returned to his. Yuuto or Rectify still didn't feel right. He was just Dan Campbell and didn't think he could consider himself by any other name. At least he got to see what he would look like to everybody else, making it easier to think of himself as Yuuto. It wasn't the first time he had to be someone else. He started putting the boots on but thought about the results of not wearing socks with boots. *Every good soldier knows foot care is essential to operating at peak efficiency,* he thought to himself. Walking back to the tree, he tore two leaves off and pictured socks just as he had the boots, and in his hands appeared a pair of socks, which had no reflection. With his feet dressed, he walked towards the house.

A dirt road passed by the side of some buildings, likely heading to a town he could not see due to the distance and the darkening evening. He walked to the front of the first building recognizing it as a home with three other buildings nearby. One looked to be a sleeping area for workers, a barn of sorts for animals, and a small blacksmith shop. Apparently, Kaito wasn't just a simple farmer; he had a lot of land and was likely a man of influence. Dan couldn't help but think, *why would these people need help?*

*

Kaito and his men had just sat down to eat together after a long day in the fields. This was the best the farm had done any of the years he knew of. In fact, the farm was doing so well that he knew he needed to get another worker but didn't know if he could spare the time it would take to go to the city and find a new worker. *If only somebody would just come to my door and ask me for work, that would fix all my problems. I just hope it's not another down on his luck or broken soldier. I have enough of those here already.* He was pulled away from

his thoughts by laughter from some of the men at the table with him.
Looking around his men, he could recall when most of them had come to
him for jobs, the majority knew nothing of farming. However, after
spending most of his life as a soldier, he took pity on those who could not
take the battle out of their souls, but here they could hopefully forget war
for a time.

He cleared his throat to get the men's attention so they could begin their
meal.

"Before we begi-." but he was interrupted by a knock at the
entrance of his home. "One moment I will see who it is," *I hope it's not
another Buddhist. I've told them I'm happy with my belief in the gods, the prosperity of
my farm is evidence of that.*

*

Dan walked to the front entrance, which was a door frame covered by a
curtain. On the door frame was a wooden plank with a wooden mallet with
which to knock. He knocked and waited some time until a man in his late
20s or early 30s appeared and seemed momentarily taken aback when he
saw Dan, who gave a deep bow.

"Noble Sir, my name is Yuuto, do you have employment for one
searching for his place in this world?"

On rising, Dan realized he was much taller than the other man and could see the top of his head.

The man returned the bow, giving the briefest indication he noticed Dan's size.

"I am Kaito, this is my land. Where are you from, and why are you here? I'm not interested in any other religions if that's why you're here."

Not another one. Kaito thought

It was all Dan could do not to laugh because he hadn't heard a phrase like that since he was a missionary in Belgium and the Netherlands. It looked like he was in the correct place.

"No, I am not here about religion, but have come from a faraway land. As a young man, I became a soldier and have fought in many battles. For my service, I was given permission to leave war behind. I now seek a peaceful life and wander; searching for purpose and peace; I believe fate has brought me here.

Oh great! Even worse, another soldier… Why me?

Kaito nodded. Disregarding the strangeness of the man's speaking.

"What do you know of farming and blacksmithing?"

Dan replied, "As a boy, I was taught of farming and blacksmithing by my father before I became a soldier."

It wasn't a complete lie. Dan's family had gardens when he was a boy, and his Dad had been a welder, which was closish.

Kaito rubbed his chin as though he were deep in thought.

But this does save me the trouble of traveling to the city.

"Hmm, fate indeed, I was just considering finding a new worker from the city. From the looks of you, I believe you to be a man of your word. If you can wield a weapon as you say, then I'm sure you can wield a farming implement, or as big as you are, pull a wagon," he said with a chuckle. He glanced at Dan's arms and said without much conviction, "We shall see tomorrow what you know of blacksmithing." He then called back into the house, "Hana, we have one more to feed."

*

Kaito motioned for him to come in, showing where he could put his sandals. Dan hadn't counted on the fact that he might have to remove his sandals. He just hoped no one would take his on accident. He wasn't sure how someone would respond. Counting his shoes, there were 13 people at dinner. Passing through another curtain, he came into a room with a long low table with 13 bowls set around; he took his seat in the one empty place.

Hopefully, he would be able to just watch everybody and do what they do. *I guess when in Ancient Japan do as the Ancient Japanese, or whoever they identify as do.* He thought to himself. Waiting a moment, he looked around at everyone as they held their bowl of what he guessed was saki up towards Kaito and quickly joined in. Then Kaito directed his bowl towards his wife, Hana, and everyone else followed suit.

"Praise and honor to she who is more beautiful than any flower and more divine than any goddess for the meal she has prepared." Hana blushed, smiled, bowed her head, and said, "Hazukashii," as they all lowered their bowls. She indeed was a beauty, she matched the beauty of any Japanese woman he had ever seen on any screen, and the way Kaito looked at her, it was clear he loved her.

"May I introduce Yuuto, a good man from far away who seeks peace. He will stay and work with us for a time." All nodded in his direction, and he nodded in return. Then each drank from their bowl as did Dan after first turning it to water with a thought. Everyone started getting rice and something else he couldn't identify. Still, it was easy enough to change it to something else. He couldn't help but think of how handy this would have been out in the field.

Hana and her two ladies excused themselves for the evening, but all the men stayed. They drank saki and shared stories until the drink ran out. Dan was used to this sort of thing in Special Forces and always had a few sealed water bottles with him. The other men were impressed at how Yuuto could hold his drink, of course, having no idea he was just drinking water. The men all looked to him expectant of some kind of story about his military or war experiences. Most of the men had fought in battles or wars, so they were very familiar with their day's tactics, which Dan wasn't. Dan had to stretch to turn his war stories into something these men could understand. His first war story had them all doubled over laughing. Apparently, Yuuto meant gentle, so they began calling him Gentle Giant. Dan made a silent note to thank Abel for his humor. He just hoped they would forget this nickname when they sobered up.

From the storytelling, he learned that Kaito was famous in the region for his swordsmanship. It was just one more reason for Dan to wonder why he was here helping a guy that seemed to have it all. Apparently, he was once a swordsman and now a blacksmith of some skill. In fact, Hana's father had been the village ruler and had one son and two daughters. Hana was the oldest daughter. The brother took over as ruler of the city when their father died, but Kaito was given Hana as a wife for a battle in which he saved the ruler's life.

Dan realized there were dimensions to this farmer far beyond farming. Still, it made sense as in early history, there were no such things as professional soldiers only citizen soldiers. Citizen soldiers did fine against other citizen soldiers, but they could not stand against professional soldiers. It had to help citizensoldiers stand firm if they knew the best among them could be rewarded with the ruler's daughter. Obviously, Kaito was more than just a citizen soldier, but he wasn't royal.

Deciding Dan was the winner of the night's drinking game, the festivities ended. The laborers stumbled to the entrance for the night. As usual, Dan was the only sober one there, so it was easy to get his sandals back on without anybody noticing. However, before he got them, he laughed because one of the men tried to put them on. In fact, everyone got a good laugh out of it. They just thought he was extra drunk. Eventually, the men made their way to the sleeping quarters, Dan practically carrying three of them. They all laid down and quickly fell asleep, save for Dan because Rectify didn't need sleep and probably couldn't have if he had tried.

CHAPTER 5
THE FIRST NIGHT

Dan realized he could go anywhere and do whatever he wanted while the

laborers slept. He could think of numerous things he could do and places

he might like to see, but he quickly remembered the things he needed to do

for this mission. The agricultural stuff would be easy to figure out, but

blacksmithing was another matter. He knew enough about welding to weld

things if needed, but blacksmithing was much different. All he knew was

that you heat the metal up and shape it with a big hammer on an anvil.

There was no telling what kind of blacksmithing was expected here. He lay

there trying to sleep, but all he could think about was Sonya. Thinking

about her was difficult because it filled him with guilt and a longing for the

future that wasn't to be. Knowing it wouldn't do him any good to lay there

thinking, he decided to find something else to do.

Leaving the laborer quarters, he silently made his way to the blacksmith shop, thankful the rain had stopped. It was covered by a roof and had three

walls. Judging by the panels hanging on the shop walls, a temporary wall

could be put up in the front if needed. Everything Dan expected to find in

a blacksmith shop was there. There was a forge and bellows that looked

different than ones he had seen in movies. There was plenty of fuel, and a

great deal of metal. The metal was unfamiliar to Dan as he looked at what

appeared to be a clump of iron and sand melted together. There were

multiple hammers hangining on the wall and an anvil near the forge. In one

corner there were several tools in need of repair. There were a few swords

on the back wall to his delight, and below them, a large chest full of sword

blades.

The swords didn't look like Samurai swords, they weren't curved. He took

one down, removing it from the sheath, he grasped the hilt, and held it up

to his eyes. The sword appeared to be made of excellent quality. The

straight blade made Dan realize he was far back in time due to the swords

very Korean design.

Wait, how do I know that? he thought to himself. He had always been

primarily interested in European swords. Then his mind was drawn back to

his Eastern Civilization class. Incredibly, he had perfect recall of it all.

Shaking his head, he went back to examining his surroundings.

On a counter, he discovered blades with more curvature that were more samurai looking. However, none were complete, and it seemed as though they were in the process of being scrapped or remade. *Kaito may be on to something here, and if I'm going to look like I know anything about blacksmithing, I better start doing something... Or maybe...* Dan muttered under his breath.

Grabbing a chunk of wood, he thought of a blacksmithing book, and it turned into blacksmithing for dummies. "Surely, there's gotta be something better." Thinking again, it turned into a book on Japanese blacksmithing with pictures; Dan smiled. *That's more like it.* He quickly read through the pages finishing it in about five minutes. He could read fast, but it still took time to turn pages. He also discovered he couldn't get paper cuts. In his haste to turn pages, he felt several times when he should have cut himself. *Well, that's going to come in handy. I wonder, am I impervious to cuts?* He grabbed a sword to experiment, but just as quickly dropped it. *Not now, I have to get to work.*

He recalled the whole book; however, there was only so much words and pictures could do. This time holding the book, he thought of a tablet with a video on traditional Japanese blacksmithing. He spent an hour watching videos on the process. They were much like YouTube only better. These were actual recordings of ancient Japanese blacksmiths. After this, the only trouble would be not to reveal too much, just assist Kaito in creating whatever he was going to develop.

Kaito had wanted to know if Yuuto knew anything about blacksmithing. Actions speak louder than words, so it was time to show that he knew blacksmithing. Taking a small piece of metal, he began hammering until it was red hot, with that, he started the tinder to heat the forge. He was sure he could blacksmith by just holding things and thinking they could be fixed, but where was the fun and sense of accomplishment in cheating? He turned to get the first tool, saw the tablet turned it back to wood before someone else accidentally found it, and threw it in the forge. It was amazing how easily and quickly, he was able to repair the tools.

The sun was just peeking over the horizon when he was on the eighth tool repair. He had gotten into a rhythm, discovering that he liked blacksmithing. However, it would've been different if he hadn't had perfect recall. Kaito's voice from behind broke him out of his rhythm.

"All that pounding… Doesn't it hurt your head?"

Dan turned to look at a Kaito, rubbing his head, evidence of a slight hangover.

"Your actions speak well for you. I see you're doing fine work, but after this one, there are seven other…" Kaitos voice trailed off when he saw the completed tools

"I wasn't tired, so I decided to get reacquainted with the forge. I

93

hope you don't mind that I helped myself to the forge and fixed all the tools."

"No… no, I don't mind at all, but how did you do all of this in one night?" Kaito picked a few of the tools up. "You not only did it fast, but you did it very well."

Dan grimaced. *Oh, great! I messed up and did too well. Hope this doesn't lead to hard to answer questions.* "I noticed that several of them weren't in terrible shape, so they were simple to fix."

"Ah, that explains things, but either way, it is most impressive, and I believe you are just the assistant I need for a project."

Dan brightened. "Are you talking about the swords? The ones on the wall are of excellent quality, I hope you don't mind I looked. It also appears you are creating a new sword. Are you having some difficulties?"

"I don't mind that you looked at the swords, and in fact, I'm glad you did. I'm trying to create a new sword that is stronger, faster, and sharper than traditional swords. Perhaps you can assist me?"

"It would certainly be my pleasure to learn at a master's hand. But tell me, how does a farmer know so much of swords?"

Kaito paused a moment before speaking.

"My father and two older brothers were the farmers, I was a soldier. My brothers were to divide the land between them, and I was sent as a youth to be part of my Lord's personal guard. I accompanied him in many battles, many were small skirmishes with the tribes people to our north. Then a warlord from the south attempted to expand into our land. My Lord was forced to call all men to war."

Kaito bowed his head to the earth, "We were victorious... but at great loss of life, leaving me as my father's only living son. I was released from my oath because of it and I saved his life. I was a friend to his son, who is now my Lord and close to his daughter Hana. Therefore, he allowed me to marry her. I learned all the basics of blacksmithing from my father as a boy. When I served my Lord, I was taught by his blacksmith in the art of making weapons. After I was released and no longer required to serve the Lord as his guard, I began making weapons for him. Now I seek to find the perfect sword, I have seen it in my dreams, but I have not been able to create it."

The dream part grabbed Dan's attention; he had always found dreams to be very important in his life.

"You have seen it in dreams? Then I take it as my duty to help you create this sword. When I first met you, I knew there was more to you than a simple farmer. I can see in your face a man who has seen war and loss. In exchange for helping you, the only payment I ask is that you allow me to assist you and teach me swordsmanship. Though I have been in many

battles, the sword was never my weapon of choice."

Kaito nodded, "We shall see if your abilities are worthy of your

price. I was going to spend the morning seeing how much you knew of

blacksmithing, but now I see you know enough. Therefore, I will show you

the farm and the work that must be done before we start work on swords."

They left and viewed all of the impressive farm. Kaito was much loved by

his men; they acted more like friends than employees. Many were former

soldiers he was trying to help. They worked the rest of the morning, and all

were impressed at Dan's strength and speed as he worked. After lunch, Dan

was headed back to the field when Kaito stopped him, instead directing him

to the smithy.

"You work too fast, and I want the others to have something to

do! Let's go work in the blacksmith shop, and then we will practice with the

sword."

No more words were needed. Both went to the forge and began by

finishing a straight sword. Dan was disappointed they were not working on

the new blades, but as he didn't want to give away any secrets, he said

nothing. He couldn't help but wonder if Kaito was the one who invented

the samurai sword, because as far as he knew, it was unknown who created the first one. Dan remembered originally, Kaito had been killed, so it couldn't possibly have been him who invented it or stolen it.

After the sword was completed, Kaito handed it to Dan in the scabbard, took another from the wall, and then directed him to walk outside the building. Attaching the swords to their waists, they walked outside and squared up against each other. It definitely didn't feel like anything he'd ever seen in a movie. First, because they weren't dressed in samurai armor but the attire of farmers. It was also strange to see Kaito wearing a straight sword, and samurai always appeared large and strong in movies.

"Yuuto, I want you to draw your sword and attack me."

"Are you sure? I don't want to accidentally cut you."

It took a few minutes for him to stop laughing. "I am very certain you will not hurt me." Kaito could still hardly keep his face straight.

Dan thought, *I'll show you.* "If you insist. I'll try and attack you. Remember, you asked for it."

Kaito's face straightened up immediately. "Stop! I did not say try, I said, attack me! Only draw your sword in the presence of another, if you intend to attack."

"In that case."

Dan was confident Kaito would be impressed because he had seen many movies and documentaries. The sword was pulled out and sliced upwards as the first move; whoever was fastest was the one who lived. He drew his sword like he had seen in movies, only the smooth fluid movement he had imagined was replaced by a clunky robotic pull of the sword from the scabbard. Before his sword was out, another was at his neck.

Kaito eyes were wide with shock and surprise. "Have you never drawn a sword before? I thought you'd fought in many battles?"

"Yes, I've been in many battles, and used numerous weapons but never a sword. Whenever I saw someone use a sword, it was already drawn."

"Ah, I understand, but the way you attempted to draw your sword is the way I drew the sword in my dream. I believe the gods have revealed this to me through you."

"Well, I'm pretty sure at least one did… but I thought you weren't interested in religion?" Dan questioned.

"Ha, I am no fool. A wise man respects the gods, but I do not concern myself in their business. Now let us continue." Kaito nodded to Dan's sword.

"Want me to try and draw my sword again?"

"No, for now I want to see what you can do once it is drawn."

Dan gripped the hilt with both hands, slightly spreading his feet with one more forward than the other as he had seen in movies and also from his knowledge of martial arts. Kaito seemed to approve as he took the same stance. The sword felt good in his hands, but he found it hard not to make lightsaber sounds as he swung it. His body felt better than it ever had before, his reflexes and strength were perfect, his first slice of the sword took Kaito by surprise. No matter how fast or strong someone is, there is much to be said about skill and experience. Kaito was able to quickly deflect it easily.

"Yuuto, that was very good! Are you sure you have never used a sword before? You have more skill than many men who have spent years using the sword, well, that is until they die against someone better."

Dan shrugged, "I am very good at observing, and I've never seriously used a sword. I find that it is always wise to conceal a few secrets from an opponent."

"It seems you are a better warrior than I imagined. This time I will attack, and I want you to deflect the blow. It would be wise if you do not try to block it, but block it."

Without warning, a blade arced directly at Dan's head. With his heightened senses and abilities, he was able to deflect and even make a counter-attack. They continued attacking and counter-attacking until it was time to eat.

Kaito smiled. "Yuuto, I have been very impressed by you today, so much so that tomorrow we will only use training swords, don't want someone to get hurt."

*

In the following weeks, farming was forgotten for Yuuto and Kaito. The mornings were spent working on Kaito's new sword design, and the evenings were spent practicing swordplay. Dan was cautious not to reveal too much about the sword. Kaito could not find a consistency he was happy with. The metal was either too hard or too soft. He was intrigued when the idea was suggested to put the more malleable metal inside the harder metal. Of course, he did not realize it had been recommended. The idea was already in his head, but hearing it from another was the verification needed to give it a try. The videos Dan had watched were very beneficial, and he found he enjoyed working with the metal.

CHAPTER 6
RAIN AND BABIES

Dan quickly became a family friend and a pseudo-bodyguard, which was very convenient, given his mission. He was honored to have a bed in the house as he became trusted like a family member, and due to his stature, he didn't fit well in the laborer's bunks. Kaito and Dan formed a bond through their mutual combat experience, a bond only a professional soldier could understand. Those who have not experienced the soldier's life and lived the hellish nightmares could never understand.

In talking to the other men, it was apparent Dan was not the only one escaping the traumas of battle. At least half of the farm laborers had fought in wars. Dan could see he was trusted more by Kaito, the bond they shared from working on the sword, and perhaps his status as Rectify was somehow felt.

Counting up the days, he found he had been here for at least a month. In that time there had been no more rain, until today, and it showed no sign

of stopping anytime soon. Even with his abilities to ignore cold and heat, it

seemed he couldn't escape the oppressive humidity. It wasn't the humidity

that affected him; it was the dreariness that all the clouds brought on and

made everything difficult for an Arizona boy, accustomed to sunny skies.

The worst part of it being overcast was the loss of visibility. This was one

of the most beautiful places Dan had ever seen. Off in the distance, there

was a dormant volcano which was now a mountain. From what Kaito said,

it last erupted in his great grandfather's time before many lived in the area.

Around the base were vast swaths of forest with a caldera on the other side,

indeed it was heaven on earth.

On a clear day, the town was partially visible from Kaito's home. The town

was a half days ride by wagon away. Asking the name of the town did no

good because all Dan could hear was a mumble. He guessed it was

something he didn't need to know because knowing might affect how he

handled things. However, he knew it was one of the largest cities this far

north. Most of the surrounding villages considered this more or less the

capital or the city they paid fealty to. Hana was from an old family

connected to many families in the surrounding area; she and Kaito were, in

fact, distant cousins. From what Dan could gather at some point in time,

the city had become like a provincial capital, and this family became the

Lords or Daimyo of the area. He smiled, for all he knew this city was Kyoto, and Hana was the sister of the Emperor.

He didn't know much about ancient Japan. He did know he must be very early in Japan's history because they did not have samurai, and their swords were straight. They also weren't tempering their blades until Dan inadvertently let slip the idea of folding the metal, and that was all it took for Kaito to run with it. Hopefully, this didn't have any kind of repercussions that shouldn't have happened yet. It's not like the secret was going to go anywhere. Kaito may have been a warrior at some point, but now he was just a farmer, and from everything he said, he was pretty determined to stay a farmer. Even more than a farmer, he had spoken at length of how much he wanted to be a father. Judging by the sounds Dan heard at night and the looks exchanged between Kaito and Hana, that might be happening soon. Assuming whatever it was, Rectify was here to fix actually got fixed. Otherwise, Kaito would be killed, and something terrible would happen to Hana.

After three days of nothing but rain, it finally stopped. Dan looked forward to getting back to making swords and practicing swordsmanship. He was getting better every day. On this day, he learned Hana's sister-in-law was pregnant, and she was due to deliver within the next month or two. Hana would start visiting to help with the delivery. Dan assumed this must be what led to Kaito trying to save her and losing his life, but he was here now, so hopefully those events wouldn't happen. It looked like the fun parts were over, and he would have to start being more Rectify than Yuuto or even Dan.

The next day while he was working with Kaito, he decided to do a little intel. The topic of Hana's trip to the city came up, so Dan took the opportunity.

"Kaito, aren't you a little worried about Hana going to the city alone?"

Kaito snorted, "I'm not crazy. I would never let her go to the city alone. Her two ladies will go with her."

Dan kept pushing. "I mean no offense, I'm sure her ladies will take care of her. But what if bandits or animals attack them?"

Kaito moved to Dan's side, speaking very softly. "I'll tell you a secret about her ladies, but you must swear on your honor and by the gods to tell no one."

One thing Dan knew about this culture and the importance of honor was that an oath of this kind was not taken lightly.

"You have my word of honor and my life that I will not reveal this secret."

Assured by Dan's promise Kaito continued.

"They were sent by her father when I married her, and they were not sent solely because of their cooking and cleaning abilities. I trained them myself in combat when I served her father. I would feel sorry for any bandit that tried to attack them." Kaito said with a huge grin.

Dan smiled, "Well, that does make me feel better, but no matter how good they are, what if they are surrounded or outnumbered? You told me many of your battles have been with the people to the north. What if they attack?"

Kaito dismissed the statement with his hand. "They would never attack three women or a small group like that. They may fight us from time to time, but they are honorable, and the fights are skirmishes, nothing more. It is a difficult situation for all, as our cities go against their lifestyle. A few times, we have disputed over land or livestock, but I do not dislike them as a people, but I will fight them when commanded."

Dan recalled mention of a warlord from the South. "What about the warlord from the south? What's to prevent him from attacking again?"

"That was years ago, and we killed his son. I do not think he will be coming back. Even if he does return, we would hear of it long before he arrived because the other villages would tell us. Besides, if he were a danger as you worry, surely, you would know his name."

Dan was caught off guard by that and stammered a moment before continuing.

"Kaito, if I know anything, it's that power-hungry men are driven by greed and revenge, and often the time to worry is when they are silent."

Kaito grunted acknowledgment. "Yes, you are correct" (all Dan heard was a mumble) "may attack again, but we will be prepared. I hope it won't be so anytime soon, but I am confident we would hear of a force marching towards our city."

Dan searched his mind for other ways to keep Hana from going or to get himself sent along to ensure nothing happened so he could get this mission finished.

Kaito touched Dan on the arm. "I'm grateful for your concern, my friend, I will send one of the men with her, though I assure you, he won't be needed."

"I thank you, my brother." But Dan thought *that's not enough*. Maybe he could watch them somehow.

Kaito ended the conversation about the journey but was not done. "She won't be leaving for two days still, but tomorrow she and I will be going into the woods to spend some time together and will be..."

Dan suspected he knew where this was going. "Whoa, I get it; you two want to be alone. That's fine, I'll stay here and take care of things."

Kaito looked down and said, "Hazukashii." The word clicked in Dan's head, he understood all languages, but it was more difficult to understand cultural norms different from his own. This time the word he heard was embarrassed. *Oh crap,* he thought to himself.

Looking away, Kaito continued to speak, "We are going for a picnic. She will be bringing her two ladies, so I thought I would bring you and Riku, who I will be sending with them to drive the wagon the next day. I don't want to be outnumbered by women, so I was hoping you would join us."

This time it was Dans turn to be embarrassed. Bowing his head in embarrassment, he stammered "I... Yes, thank you, I would like to join you."

There wasn't much left to say or do that night, so after more practicing, all except for Rectify went to bed. If he wasn't going to be able to go with Hana tomorrow, maybe there was a way he could watch without them knowing, but he doubted he could make two copies of himself. He thought for a while until suddenly, he was struck with an idea.

Somehow, God sees all, and while I undoubtedly can't, nor would I want to see all, maybe my new abilities can help? I could make a piece of wood into a tablet to see her surroundings, but even if it looked like a wooden block to everyone else, it would seem strange for him to walk around all day, staring at a piece of wood. Perhaps it's time to test my newly expanded brain.

Dan had always imagined his brain as a library or databank with multiple rooms and shelves or computer servers. As he lay there, contemplating mental functions, the realization he hadn't been using his mental abilities to their full extent came to his mind. He created a visual screen in his mind enabling him to look all around the room with his eyes, yet, somewhere in his consciousness, see this screen. It was like he had split his mind, yet it was whole. He could explain it no more than he could explain how any of his other senses worked. While he could see the screen, it remained blank. He guessed he had to command it mentally. He commanded it with his mind. *Screen, you will show me Hana, at all times.*

Instantly the screen flicked on and showed Kaito and Hana awake lying very close to each other. *Oh, crap! Screen stop! You will show me, Hana, only if she is in danger.*

He still needed to get used to these new abilities, but at least he had learned he didn't have to stay awake all night. He thought, *go to the next day at dawn,* and instantaneously, the darkness disappeared, and sunlight was peeking over the horizon. He smiled; he had never liked the need for sleep, food, and the other functions.

CHAPTER 7
A SIMPLE PICNIC

The next morning they set off heading towards the grove where Rectify

first appeared. They went farther north into the woods by the extinct

volcano and found a peaceful clearing. It was a beautiful day, and according

to the men at the farm, the rainy season was over. The birds were singing

overhead and bugs were buzzing through the air.

It felt like any picnic Dan had ever been on, but he couldn't remember

when he had last been on one. The food was good, and all were having a

pleasant time talking and laughing. Suddenly, the hair on the back of his

neck stood on end, and the screen in his mind for Hana flicked on. The

birds stopped singing, and the horse not yoked to the wagon started

running. The others had also detected the sudden change. A commotion

came from the direction of the woods.

Ok, this must be it, he thought to himself, drawing his sword. Yet reaching with all of his senses, he could detect no enemies. Then from the woods came a loud rustling from which emerged a brown bear. Dan immediately thought of a grizzly bear, but it looked slightly different in the skull from the ones he had seen. It was young, maybe half-grown, but it was bigger than a black bear. It would have been taller than Dan had it stood. It was easily large enough to kill someone, especially when frightened and enraged, as it was, running with arrows sticking out of its flanks.

He was immediately struck with the thought, *this must be how Kaito died, and why Hana was left in a situation to be taken, or whatever was to happen.* Kaito took a position in front of Hana sword drawn, directly in the bear's path. Dan and Riku both went running to Kaito's side to try and protect him from the bear. Before they could get close enough to do anything, the bear fell to the ground as five or six arrows came from the woods striking it nearly simultaneously. Ten men slowly came walking out of the woods with their hands up showing they were weaponless, having left their bows in the woods. Kaito eased his guard, putting his sword away, while Riku and Dan tensed, ready for an attack.

"Put your weapons away; I believe this is part of their religion. Though I do not know why they are here? I speak a little bit of their language, perhaps I can find out," Kaito said to his men. Both instinctively obeying him.

They looked and dressed differently from the other Japanese people Dan

had met. There were slight similarities. They seemed to have lighter skin

and thicker beards, though not as long as the pictures he remembered

seeing in his old textbooks. On average, they were a few inches taller and

had larger frames than the laborers at the farm, though still not as big as

him. Thinking more of his cultural anthropology studies in college, he

remembered reading about the Ainu. They were the indigenous people of

Japan.

As was the story throughout the history of the world, the indigenous people

were slowly pushed out. In this case, north to the island of Hokkaido, and

mostly assimilated into the conqueror's culture. Dan decided he was in

Japan before they were forced all the way north and assimilated.

The men continued walking towards the bear, hands still held out to show

they meant peace. Kaito never moved; he just stood still, continually

watching the men. Dan marveled at the impassivity on Kaito's face, though

impossibly outnumbered, he showed no fear. He was like a lion on the

Serengeti, confident in his ability and not about to let any other predator

know he was worried about them. One of the Ainu, who looked much

younger than the rest, possibly only 12, pulled out a knife and rushed to the

bear, which was not yet dead, and sliced it across the throat, ending its slow

blood loss.

One of the older men in the group who looked to be a leader, and a few years older than Kaito, walked past the boy who had just killed the bear. Speaking to Kaito in broken Japanese, which, combined with the broken words Kaito knew of their language, enabled them to communicate. This exchange was also the only time Kaito showed any signs of nervousness. Dan only knew by the slight relaxing of his shoulder blades. Aside from this display, there were no other indications, and conversations ensued. Neither man knew that Dan could understand their every thought and word. The hunting of the bear was part of a religious ceremony called Lomante in which they return the Bear God back to his home as they believed the gods possessed the forms of animals on earth.

Dan gathered, this group had been cast out by their people due to being wrongfully accused but said nothing of what the accusation was. Dan had a feeling whatever it was, they were truthfully innocent and willing to work with the Japanese treating them in the same manner with which they were treated. They were originally from much farther north but had settled in the woods near the extinct volcano after their banishment. They fled in the night and took the village's bear for this ceremony because they had raised it. They felt it was the last time they would find this type of bear needed to do the ritual. This last part was said with melancholy and a sadness that only comes from someone who has or will lose an essential piece of who they are.

Somehow the bear had managed to escape from their encampment, and they needed to finish their ritual, thus the chase through the woods. Dan could sense that the younger boy with them had faltered in doing his duty with the bear. The adults were trying not to accuse the boy for his mistake in front of Kaito and his group. Dan also couldn't deny the nagging feeling or reminder of divine help. Regardless of why they were here, or how this meeting came about, Dan was impressed by their exceptional accuracy with the bow. He was drawn away from thinking about the impressive display when he recognized a misunderstanding forming between Kaito and the other leader.

After the initial shock of realizing just how much he could understand and feel from the two participants, he walked quickly to their side, hoping to calm the situation. Walking towards the two, Dan's attention was suddenly drawn back to the woods from which the bear and the Ainu had appeared. He was shocked to see armed men in black that had been invisible to him previously. It was only his exaggerated abilities that allowed him to detect them. As they were attempting to be stealthy and not make any movements, he did not draw attention to their presence. They were part of the Ainu contingent, evidenced by the man doing the talking and the subtle signals he was making with his hand, signaling the dark-clad individuals to stay back. Forgetting the others for the moment, he focused on the matters at hand.

"Friends, excuse my interruption, but may I be of assistance? I believe a misunderstanding is occurring, and I can help."

Both men turned to look at him and then just as quickly looked back at each other shocked that Dan had just spoken to both of them at the same time in their native language. The leader of the Ainu was perplexed that an outsider could be so fluent in their language. At the same time, Kaito was confused the leader was able to understand Yuuto so well. He was Ainu and, assuredly, Yuuto could not speak Ainu, being from the south. Both men bowed, indicating they accepted his intrusion.

Dan started by asking each man, in turn, what they were trying to say, and what they were hearing. Kaito was angry because he felt the other man was saying they had ruined their ceremony. The Ainu had cursed him by his gods and demanded payment for the bear and ruining their ceremony. The other man was equally angered because he felt that Kaito demanded that he be paid for the ordeal.

Things were quickly settled as Dan translated and explained what the other was trying to say. In the end, a type of alliance was created, with each giving their oath to the other. Kaito would help them by interceding on their behalf with the Lord of the village. He would provide them with food and

any basic needs they might have. In return, the Ainu vowed that they would

offer assistance in any way Kaito asked. Kaito recognized their skill with the

bow and had never been one to turn down hunting and military skills.

Kaito and Dan agreed to send Dan with the Ainu to ascertain their needs

and find the horse that ran off, if possible. Of course, it went without

saying, scout and report on their combat readiness and military possibilities.

Dan returned with the Ainu to their encampment, though it was only a five

or ten-minute walk. He noted it was a challenging area to navigate with

roots and rocks protruding from the ground. He was also acutely aware,

due to his heightened senses, that the dark-clad individuals were on all sides

escorting them, though never visible to the naked eye. He made it a point

not to look in the direction of the individuals, as he didn't want to make it

evident that he wasn't an average human. Still, it certainly did make him

wonder about every ninja movie he had ever seen. He wouldn't have been

shocked if they were big walking turtles, ready to say "cowabunga dude!"

He was pulled from his musings when a firm hand on his shoulder, jerking

him back quickly brought him back to the present. His reflexes responded,

and he reached for the hand on his shoulder, twisted the arm as he turned

and struck out with his other hand to hit the person in the chest. They

slipped his strike taking it instead on the shoulder. Dan checked himself as soon as he realized what had happened and apologized energetically.

He and the Ainu leader both looked surprised, Dan, because the man could slip his strike and the other man was equally surprised to find a man faster than him. The man pointed to a trap on the ground, which Dan had been about to step on. Looking up, Dan discovered many bows and weapons pointed at him. All went back to normal once the situation was understood, and they continued to their encampment.

Dan was impressed by the village's orderliness and how clean and industrious all were. Many women were weaving types of cloth that looked like the clothing of the men Dan was with. Their dwellings were constructed of thatch and wood. Each building appeared to have an animal pen and its own garden area. They had cleared all trees from this area, but it was apparent they had not been here long because several buildings were still in progress, and it did not yet stink of animal manure.

Dan was taken to a dwelling in the center of the village. Judging by the broken animal pen attached to it, this was where the bear had been kept and was likely the home of their leader. Once inside, he was directed to a bed at the end of the room where an aged woman appeared gaunt, coughing loud and often.

The Leader went to the old woman, whispered something in her ear, then placed his forehead to hers. As he turned back, his eyes glistened with moisture.

"Yuuto, this is my mother, the elder of our village and family. She is very sick and suffers from the effects of the fire, which killed my father."

Dan detected equal parts sorrow and anger in his expression, indicating the fire had been relatively recent and was more than just an accident. His heart immediately went out to this man's mother; somehow, even though his grandma wasn't remotely Asian, he could imagine her in the same feeble condition. His blood boiled to think she was in this shape because of another's evil act, but his compassion for helping women won over his anger. He felt a tear fall down his cheek; if this were his mother, he wouldn't be able to contain all of his feelings. He would, of course, be by her side as soon he could, and after she was taken care of, he would find the responsible party and well…

Both men stood there, watching and listening to her cough and struggle for each breath. A pang of guilt hit him. It was his mission to help women, these feelings of revenge and hate were somehow inappropriate He replaced his thoughts with justice, mercy, and compassion for this woman, and justice by delivering the culprits to these people.

To his mind came a lesson he had been taught in church. Some boys were walking out in the desert when one of them was struck by a rattlesnake.

The boys spent time chasing the snake down and took revenge by killing it.

They returned to their friend, but before getting him medical attention, he

died from the venom coursing through his veins. Looking down at her, he

knew he could do something to help her right now. He was the first to

break the silence. He wasn't sure how to word it, so he just went for it.

"I…I have power entrusted to me by… well, I can help your

mother if you believe I can."

The leader stopped for a moment, reaching his hand to his beard

unconsciously stroking it as he thoughtfully looked in his mother's direction

for 10 or 15 seconds. His silence was accentuated by the rhythmic sound of

someone chopping wood outside. Finally, he looked straight at Dan and

tried to speak for a few moments before in a subdued voice, he was able to

reply.

"I believe you! I know there are higher powers, and who am I to

tell the Gods what they can and can't do. I have watched you move with a

speed that no man should be capable of. You can understand and do things

which should be impossible. I know you spoke two languages at once, even

though you tried to hide it. When you saw my men in the woods, you were

not surprised, and those men have spent lifetimes perfecting their stealth

abilities. I possess those same abilities, yet I cannot even detect them when they do not want to be seen. I will not ask who you are, but I believe all you say, so yes, I believe you can help my mother."

Dan patted the man's shoulder as he walked towards his mother, giving him a slight head nod. Kneeling by the ailing woman's side, he placed his hands on her head, closed his eyes, and offered a silent prayer for permission to heal her. A smile crossed his lips when in his head and heart, permission was heard and felt. He was never sure exactly where it came from but knew he heard the desired answer. With permission granted, he proceeded to heal her. Within seconds of removing his hands and standing, she opened her eyes. Then she looked at Dan, sat up, leaned over the side of the bed, and with one great cough, a black glob landed on the floor. For a moment, she sat silently, looking at what had come out of her mouth. Her son making an audible gasp. She wasted no time in motioning her son to her side.

"He is the one! First son, this man is your brother, and my second son, he may have anything he wishes. There is no secret too secret for him to know."

Her son stammered for a moment.

"All secrets?"

Her only answer was a nod.

Dan was struck silent. He hadn't anticipated this at all; he just thought he would help these people and be on his way to the next mission. Now it appeared this mission was becoming even more complicated.

The man walked back to Dan, amazement on his face. "Brother, follow me, I will teach you the legacy of our family, and why we are here."

Before turning to follow his new brother, Dan walked to his newly adopted mother and careful not to kneel in the black glob, took her hand, speaking with his head bowed.

"Mother, though you are not the mother of my birth, and the mother of my birth will always be most honored and loved in my heart, I swear to hold you in equal esteem. I am honored to be considered your son. You are an honorable woman and family. I will give my life to defend you and your honor. I am at your call, and will always fight for honor and justice."

After pledging, he looked up to see her looking into his eyes as though she could see his innermost parts. Not letting go of his hand, she leaned forward, touching her head to his just as she had before with her son.

"Our family is honored by the one."

Dan wondered, *What does she mean by "the one"?*

She let go of his hand, Dan guessed that meant he was dismissed. He walked to the exit where his new brother was waiting. Exiting the home, the leader of the Ainu pointed to two of the women near the house, directing them to attend to their mother by calling them sister and cousin.

Dan thought it strange that he didn't call them by name, but assumed he would learn names soon enough. Walking towards the forest opposite the side of the village he entered on, they came to a clearing after several minutes. Men and boys were practicing the bow and varying types of armed and unarmed combat, which seemed familiar to Dan.

All stopped mid-motion the moment they saw a stranger in their midst. The silence was broken when the leader held his hand up to introduce Dan to the group.

"This man is now my brother and my mother's second son. You will keep no secret from him. He is Ak Yuuto," which Dan heard in his head as a younger brother Yuuto.

After the announcement, all bowed in Dan's direction and then returned to their tasks as though it was a daily occurrence. All except for one man standing in the center of the unarmed fighting area who scoffed loud enough for all to hear. Dan and the leader both turned to look at him. The leader huffed, "have something to say, cousin?" Evidently, there was a history between the two.

"Yes, who is this man that we should accept him and teach him our secrets?"

The leader grimly replied, "My mother!... The leader of our clan."

"Pah, you expect us to accept him just because a dying woman declared it so? When your father died, mine should have led the clan as he was second oldest."

"Cousin, this has already been discussed. My mother is our leader as she is the oldest living member of our clan as our fathers and the others all perished in the fire. The clan decided you would not lead; you must accept that, or do you want to decide by combat with me."

The cousin faltered after that and reconsidered his argument.

"This man is a foreigner, can he even fight? For all you know, he's working with the enemy!"

The leader was clearly angry but still practicing control.

"I vouch for him, and I tell you now he is my brother and my mother who has recovered thanks to this, my brother has declared it so!"

"Fools! If you believe and trust in him so much then I will decide by combat, but with this outsider." He said, pointing at Dan. "Can he even speak our language?"

The leader stepped forward as though to fight, but was stopped when Dan put his hand on his shoulder. The cousin was astonished to learn that Dan could speak their language when he spoke.

"Cousin, I accept your challenge. What are your conditions? If it is to the death, then I assure you I still accept the challenge."

The cousin was taken aback by that.

"Death um no, of course not, but," he said, trying to sound confident "when I win I lead the clan."

"Ah, and if I win?" Dan asked.

"Ha, if you win? If you win, I may never challenge or speak of challenging again."

"In that case, let us begin." Dan moved to a defensive position.

The man facing him adopted a similar stance then rushed at Dan with a punch he easily blocked, followed by a flurry of more fists all successfully blocked. The man raged with anger and ran in one more time, this time Dan grabbed his clothes and used his momentum to fling him across the yard. Not turning around, Dan asked if he surrendered yet. His only answer was the sound of him running back at him. Dan turned around just as the cousin tried to kick him in the back of his head. He caught his foot then stepped on the foot he still had on the ground. Holding his opponent in a perpetual split, his opponent looked at him with a mix of shock and pain.

"Do you surrender yet?

"Youll have to finish me cow..." the word coward was cut off when Dan punched him in the groin. As he lay on the ground in the fetal position moaning, the leader told him to moan if he surrendered. Then he declared the fight over.

The men all looked on in amazementas Dan and the leader left the fighting area.

They stood at the edge of the training area for several moments, watching the men before the leader spoke only loud enough for Dan to hear.

"What do you call your type of fighting?"

Dan looked over and smiled. "Winning."

The leader laughed at that and then became serious.

"Perhaps you wonder why I have not yet told you my name? I am Sikanna." Which Dan understood in his mind to mean dragon.

"We do not speak our names lightly, they are sacred. We only say our name to the family, and then rarely, which is why we refer to one another by our family position. No outsider is permitted to know our name, for our name is our honor, but we have an outsider name should we have to trade with outsiders. It is only give it when required. Any person that hears our true name, either becomes family or must die."

Dan nodded his head once, promising their secrets were safe with him on his life. He determined with this knowledge, he would share his correct name.

"Yuuto is not my true name, I will tell you my name, but it is not time for others to know. I am Rectify, and I am here to fix wrongs that have been and will be done unless I stop them."

Sikanna smiled at this news.

"It as our mother said, you are the one!"

There it was again; now seemed like the best time for Dan to ask. "What exactly does she mean that I'm the one?"

Sikanna was silent for a moment, contemplation visible on his face. "Our mother is a woman of deep insight and powerful dreams. She dreamed some time ago of an outsider who was to come and restore our family's honor. Her dream is what brought us to this place, and is why we took the bear that initiated our meeting. She saw in her dream that the bear was key to receiving help from the gods. However, I did not expect an outsider to be the tool of the gods."

Dan tried not to smile, but he just couldn't help it.

"God... the gods move in a mysterious way. If I am the one, then on my honor, I will do my best to do my duty." He had to make a conscious effort not to say the Scout Oath.

As they walked through the woods, Sikanna told the story of how the family had come to be in their present state; it was a long tale. Their honor and combat secrets were more important than their lives, and they promised to teach him their secrets. However, the things he had seen and heard gave him some ideas about who or what these people were or might become. He put that to the back of his mind, intent on listening to the story.

The husband to one of Sikanna's, now Dan's, sisters had betrayed the family. He set the fire that killed Sikanna's father, uncles, and most of their leaders and almost killed his mother. It was an attempt to take over the family, so he could reveal their secrets to outsiders for gain. Before his plot could be completed, he was caught and tortured until he explained why he had done it.

A Japanese man named Koukai from far to their south conspired with him. In exchange for their secrets, this Koukai would support him in becoming chief of all Sikanna's people. They would then form an alliance and destroy Kaito's kingdom, then the two peoples would have eternal peace as they conquered all their neighbors. They were told he was a servant of a man named Kaito, an evil man who must be killed before attacking the city so there could be peace.

Sikanna finished the long story. "Had Kaito truly been evil, we would have killed him, but we watched him and saw that this was a lie—"

"Wait!" Dan interrupted. "The bear escaping wasn't an accident, was it? You and your men were in the woods to kill Kaito, weren't you?"

Sikanna shrugged the questions off, "The bear escaping truly was an accident, but served to show Kaito's heart. An evil man would not have placed himself between his woman and a bear. As for the rest..." he shrugged, "Kaito lives..." then he continued his story as though there had been no interruption.

"For my brother-in-law's crimes against the family, he was put to death. The rest of the people did not know our secrets and, therefore, not knowing the extent of his sin, cast us out. They swore should our family be seen again, they would declare war on us, despite all we have done to

protect them for generations."

The brother-in-law had already taught some of their secrets to this Koukai.

Now they were here to restart their lives and find and kill the man named

Koukai at any cost to protect their secrets. The conversation finished, Dan's

training in the family secrets began.

CHAPTER 8
A NEW START

It had been a week since Dan met his new family and learned of their

secrets. Kaito had already started taking food to them and occasionally

received some game in return. Their most significant contribution was

scouting around the land for any sign or word of Koukai. Kaito was

informed that the kingdom in the south was actively plotting, so he was

pleased to have their help, but only Dan knew the Koukai part. Dan

convinced Kaito of their reliability and value as military allies. Surprisingly

Kaito permitted him to make weapons for them, though he stressed they be

made of the old straight blades of which many were nearly completed.

However, he told him if he wanted to forge a new sword aside from the

one Kaito made for himself, he could.

Kaito and Dan had continued to practice, and with the new skills Dan had

learned with Sikanna on his few visits during the week, he was getting better. He knew Kaito had noticed his sudden gain of ability, though he said nothing. However, Dan suspected his sudden increase in skills somehow had something to do with why Kaito had agreed to give them weapons.

Dan was in the smithy, working on a new sword for Sikanna and was very pleased with its progress. He hadn't used any of his abilities with it. He was just about to start sharpening it when Kaito came in to begin their daily sparring session. Dan hated to quit but gave in knowing Kaito was excited to get things done. Hana was due to return from helping her sister-in-law prepare for her pregnancy today. She would come back to visit for two days and then return to the city until the baby was delivered, and her sister-in-law was all settled.

Dan was glad, but also perplexed. He hadn't expected to be here this long. He was sure something would've happened to Hana because of her visit to the city. He had continuously monitored the screen in his mind for any signs of danger but hadn't seen anything alarming. Walking through the smithy door while tying on his practice sword, he checked the screen one more time. They were only 10 or 15 minutes away. He was confident nothing could happen to her now, especially with his new family watching the surrounding area.

He and Kaito greeted each other in their makeshift arena as they did every day. Knowing they didn't have much time, Dan focused all of his attention

on the duel. Dan made the first attack with a downward strike, which Kaito

quickly blocked and then attempted to slide his blade towards Dan. Dan

quickly dodged his stomach back, and this time made an upward slice from

the left side, which Kaito barely blocked. The fight continued with one

attacking and the other parrying then countering with his own attack. Kaito

had told him a few nights earlier during their evening meal that he believed

they were now equal in skill, though he stressed, not experience. Dan, along

with all the other men seated at the table, laughed as though it were a jest.

However, every time they dueled, the men stopped working and gathered

around to watch, suggesting to an outside observer that it was a good fight.

Both combatants were utterly unaware of the crowd formed around them.

Both were drenched in sweat, despite being shirtless and cooled by a light

breeze. The fight was wholly equal neither man looked to have the

advantage. All knew it was only a question of who made the first mistake.

Then in the blink of an eye, the fight was over with Dan holding his sword

two inches away from Kaito's neck. The surrounding men were silent, to

see the greatest swordsman any had ever seen defeated. Kaito was the first

to speak, and surprisingly to all, he seemed cheerful when he spoke.

"Ah, I've been waiting for this moment a long time. It has been a

very long time since I was defeated, the last time I was just a child. I am very pleased to find someone of my same skill level. For it is only through being challenged that we become better. I'll have to put in some effort next time."

Dan just snorted. Both men lowered their swords. As Kaito put his away, he looked to the road and began running. Dan and the rest of the men turned as well, expecting some sort of trouble. But instead, they saw Hana returning in the wagon. She leaped from the wagon into Kaito's arms, and he carried her back to their home. Dan and the others went back to their work or found something else to do; each was certain they would not be having dinner in the house tonight.

Dan returned to the smithy. When certain no one could hear him, he released his pent-up excitement.

Raising his fist into the air, he exclaimed, "That's how it's done!" Then in his best Darth Vader voice, he quoted the famous line, "Once I was the learner, now I am the master." He couldn't help laughing at himself and being filled with joy.

He happily got back to the sword he had been working on, but, in his excitement, forgot all about trying to do it without his abilities. He took the unfinished sword and made it appear as he pictured in his mind; it looked good. He decided it wouldn't hurt to make a few more. He spent the rest of the night making swords to Kaito's new design using all the blacksmithing

he had learned and his "Rectify" abilities. By the time the sun went down,

he had made 12 swords and realized they would be hard to explain. He put

all the swords in the chest and left them, deciding he would figure out how

to explain them later.

He returned to the house as quietly as possible and lay down on his bed.

Usually, he would just make time pass until the sun came up, but was too

excited tonight. Though he didn't exactly know about this whole Rectify

thing, so far, it felt like he hadn't done what he was here to do. Sure he had

done some good and learned Japanese sword fighting from a legitimate

master, which was worth something. Sure, he wished he hadn't died. He

had always imagined getting 20 or 25 years in the service and then retiring

doing who knows what. He had always been confident, at least hoped he

would've been able to marry Sonya. They had an unspeakable bond. He

knew no matter what, after his time as Rectify, he would make things better

for her, and someday, somehow, they would be together again.

With his thoughts on Sonya, he suddenly smacked his head and softly said.

"I'm a complete idiot!"

If he had so much use of his brain and was able to watch Hana in one part

of his mind and still focus on what was at hand. Why couldn't he do the same with Sonya or any of his family members? He quickly made screens for whoever he could think of, amazed he could view them all at once. His family was doing well, even his parents; he knew they missed him, but they were doing well otherwise. He was most surprised to see what Sonya had been up to since his death. He had never been able to share with her or anyone all he did, but when she learned some of what he did and why he did it, it changed her.

She stayed in Arizona for a few months, then moved to Bethesda, Maryland, where she became a volunteer at Walter Reed National Military Medical Center. During his career, he spent as much as he could on life insurance and investments. They were all in his parent's name because he didn't care about money when he was on active duty. Everything was based on the idea that he would have all the money he needed when he retired and married Sonya. But just in case, he wanted to make sure they were very comfortable in their remaining years. He was pleased with the way his mother was handling the money. She was doing exactly as he had asked her in his final letter. Some went to his church, some to a scholarship fund for his local high school for students going to Eastern Arizona College. Above all, he asked his mom to give Sonya as much as she needed to fulfill her dreams. Sonya used some money to move to Maryland, and on top of her volunteering, she began nursing school.

He was indescribably happy to see her happy and doing so well. She seemed to be making friends and keeping herself busy. He couldn't help but smile watching her. He shed a few tears thinking back on their past and reflecting on the pang of guilt he felt at his funeral for holding her back. *Oh Sonya, I'm so sorry I left you, and that you will have to go on without me for so long.*

He comforted himself, just as he had waited for Sonya, she would wait for him. He knew someday after everything was over, they would be together again. On this happy thought, he felt the excitement stirring inside him again, and felt like he had a new start. Sonya was and always would be his inspiration. He felt more determined than ever to do his duty as Rectify the Avenging Angel. He would let nothing stop him, but wasn't sure he could think of himself as anything but just Dan Campbell, on another deployment. With this new determination, he closed his eyes to the dark and opened them again to sunlight.

The next two days were quiet. He didn't feel the need to stay close to his charges, knowing he could watch them with his mind. Additionally, with his Ainu family scouting the area, he was confident no assailants could harm Kaito or Hana. He decided to take a walk and test out some of his new abilities. Taking his new sword, he walked towards the extinct volcano on the other side of Sikanna's village. He started out walking, advanced to jogging, and ended up in an all-out sprint, running like he was back on the field carrying the ball to the end zone. Only he wasn't getting tired. It felt as

though he could run like this forever. Yet he still didn't feel like he was

reaching his full speed; with a little thought and determination, he found

another gear doubling his speed. The trees he ran past were a blur, yet he

was able to slip past and dodge every obstacle encountered.

He was a big fan of Star Wars, and of course, the superpowered jumping

was something every kid imagined being able to do. As he ran, it was like he

knew his path before reaching it. No rock or tree could surprise him

because before reaching them, he had already reacted. It wasn't long after

this discovery that he grew bored and, with an accidental thought, found

himself atop the extinct volcano he was running towards. He was stunned.

How in the heck did I get up here?

He would never have admitted to being afraid of heights, just cautious.

Walking towards the edge with trepidation because of that caution, he

wasn't prepared for the sight before him. The surrounding countryside's

beauty was breathtaking, overpowering any fear or caution; remembering he

couldn't die also helped. All before him was green—trees stretched out in

all directions. There was a great valley around the volcano base with a lake

fed by many streams to one side that must've been formed by a volcanic

eruption in the past. One river led away from the lake, which crossed under

a bridge between Kaito's farm and the city. That river must've been why the town was so challenging to see at times because of fog. There were trees all along the river save for where they had been cleared on either side of the bridge.

The water was clear and blue as the summer sky. The few small clouds suggested the rainy season was over just as everyone at the farm had said. Up until this point, Dan had only grumbled about the humidity because while he didn't feel weather effects, he still felt their gloom. He couldn't help hating rain and moisture. The annoyances were ingrained in his dry Arizona soul. Even if his time in the Navy and the Allied Special Forces had necessitated his adaptation to the wet, he still hated it. However, despite the discomfort, the sight from here made it all worth it. The vibrant view before him was breathtaking.

In the distance stood a lone yellow hill, not yellow because it was dry, but yellow because it was covered by flowers. He stood there trying to determine his feelings about all before him, and for the first time, really thinking about what it meant to be Rectify. When he first came to Japan, he thought it would be a few days of fun; do some sword fighting, save the day, and then move on like it was just another action movie. Now, after seeing Sonya the night before, he was thinking more deeply than he had since he died. Like everything else in life, important things take dedication and time, and he was always one to take the time, so why did it take him so long to see that now?

Looking over the surrounding land, his thoughts moved beyond himself. Slowly surveying the mountain's surroundings, he found the farm, followed the relatively straight road leading to the city, crossed the bridge, and then found the city. It was larger than he had imagined and much more organized than he could have expected. A palace, which was more of a large house surrounded by a wall 2 or 3 times as tall as a man, stood in the center. Surrounding the palace, the streets and homes radiated out in concentric squares.

Spreading from the city were small groupings of homes around farms or other necessities for civilization. All of these smaller groups of homes contributed to something more significant than themselves, just like his mission as Rectify. Take one small piece out of the equation, and the city and the people he was to help would suffer. He thought of his big-picture mission, which was for Sonya. He didn't know how but all these little missions must somehow contribute to the whole. He knew this mission had to be necessary even if he couldn't see how. He accepted being Rectify without hesitation so he could fix things for Sonya. He was confident if he could have stopped that one event in her life from happening, things would be different, and they could be together and have a family.

Now, considering all the lives before him in the surrounding countryside, he felt guilty for his selfishness. So many people in the history of the world have been wronged; it wouldn't be right for Sonya to be the only person to have the help of Rectify. Rectify should not view one person as more important than any other. Yet, he was doing all this for Sonya because, in his mind, she was more important than almost anyone else; she and his mom were in a close tie, but of course, she won. She wasn't one of the names on his mission list to help, but it went without saying that if she weren't meant to be helped, he wouldn't be here now.

Just as a sudden gust of air moved his hair, he thought back to something Abel had said before he ever started as Rectify.

I will always be me, from the beginning to the end. I have been and always will be Rectify. Looking up to the sky, his left hand automatically searched for his knife until he remembered he didn't have it anymore. He asked questions every thinking person asks at some point. *Who am I? Who was I before I became Dan Campbell?* In his mind, he heard *Rectify*. Again. he thought, *after all this is done, who will I be?* He heard *Rectify*.

I have been and always will be Rectify? I'm not just some guy that happened to fit the position because I was available, it's me?

A smile crept across his face. He was someone important, even if he didn't know how or why. But whoever he was before must've been someone awesome, so he better not let that guy down. Which meant he needed to decide now what he needed to do to be Rectify. The only thing he could think to do here at this high quiet place was to pray. Sure, he had a constant connection with heaven, but he hadn't prayed like he used to in a long time and felt like he had been missing it. He still had more questions than answers about what he could do as Rectify.

He had always considered himself a medieval knight with the same code of honor. His desire to be a knight was so ingrained that when he prayed before any military, combat, or rescue mission, he knelt with his rifle like it was a knight's sword, and now here he was with a real sword. Drawing it from the scabbard, he very gently placed the tip of the sword on the ground, blade facing away from him. Going to one knee, he closed his eyes to pray. He poured out his soul, with no thought of time. He wanted help to be Rectify and needed help knowing what to do.

A feeling came that it would become much more complicated than he expected, and he would soon learn more of who he was. As always, he felt the assurance that he would get the help he needed at the right time, but not before. A familiar feeling returned, which he had felt many times when he prayed before, during, and after combat. It was different this time; aside from that familiar feeling came a voice from behind him, he recognized the voice.

"Dan, Rectify, or whatever you may be called, God knows who you are, no matter what name is used."

Dan stood returning his sword to it's scabbard and turned to look at Abel, who had appeared behind him.

"Abel, I didn't expect you to show up here. I was just starting to-."

Abel held his hand up to stop him.

"Yes, I know, but more importantly," pointing upward, "He knows. He knows before you ask. He will speak to you when you are ready. For now, I am His messenger. This is," again pointing up, "His message."

"Dan, I have known you longer than mortal man can comprehend. I have been watching you, and though you are not perfect, you are Rectify, and only you can do this because long before you can remember, you chose to be Rectify. I know your innermost feelings; I know your fears and your joys. You fear you are not good enough. You fear for your family and the one you love. I also know fear, for I have suffered as no mortal can. But because of faith and love I would not stop what I did for you and for all. Pay no mind to your loved ones, for I am with them and protect them. Do not spend your time dwelling on the living! Do your duty, and leave the rest to me! Soon your questions will be answered, but be careful! You will face enemies who are not what they appear. They will know things you have forgotten. You have much ahead of you; Kaito, Hana, Japan, and all the world are depending on you!"

Dan's eyes grew large when he heard the world was depending on him.

"What? But how is the world depending on me?"

Abel shook his head

"That's the end of the message for now. I will tell you this, if we told you all the details, you would never have to consider a decision because you would do it without thought. In all things, you must make your own decisions after learning the facts. If you cannot make a decision, you aren't truly free, and freedom is power. Trust me, you don't want to know, and you'll thank me someday. You have been entrusted with great power. You don't need to ask permission to do things; He trusts you to choose well. Now rise up, don't worry about unimportant things—God is with you! He is always watching over you, and He loves you. Now, we all have things to do, and if you'll notice it's getting late, so sayonara!" Abel turned to leave then quickly turned back, his hand behind his back. "Oh, I have something I think you'll recognize," he said, holding something in his hand Dan indeed recognized.

Dan looked up at Abel speechless. "I made a few changes to your knife. It's now indestructible."

Smiling, Dan took it and could only stare. Taking it out of the sheath to examine it, he was overwhelmed with feelings and memories.

"But how do you have this? It was supposed to be given to Sonya."

Abel gave him a kind and sad look.

"In all the commotion, your knife got left behind, and they weren't able to go back and get it because, well, things happened, and they weren't able to go back. We knew how important it was to you, so we got it for you. For what it's worth, I'm sorry they weren't able to get it to her."

Dan only half-listened to Abel, but he understood all too well that things did indeed happen. He was so focused on the knife, didn't notice Abel had disappeared as quietly as he appeared.

Still in complete shock from seeing his treasured knife again, Dan asked a question as he lifted his head.

"Will there be a way to get it back to Sonya someday?"

But he saw that Abel was gone.

I guess I'll have to ask next time, he thought to himself.

Dan didn't want his visit to end but knew it was over, and he had things to do. After a few moments thinking about all he had just heard and of his feelings, he looked up and was shocked to see the moon low in the sky. The stars were coming to life and reflecting off the lake in front of him. He could've stayed there taking it all in forever but knew he better get to the farm before it grew too late or they would be looking for him. He checked that his sword was in its scabbard, then smiled with newfound confidence.

I am Rectify, he thought, closing his eyes. When he opened them an instant later, a smile crossed his face, and he walked into the front of Kaito's house, ignoring the faint voice in the back of his head saying, *You are just Dan.*

CHAPTER 9
PREPARING FOR A BABY

Morning came just like any other, save for one difference: Dan had actually

slept instead of blinking the night away. He stopped worrying about what

his family and Sonya were doing. With his mind cleared of distractions, he

was able to focus on his roles as Rectify and Yuuto. Until his work was

finished, he wasn't Dan Campbell; he was Rectify the Avenging Angel.

Rectify smiled because someone very soon was going to wish they had

never been born. Just as soon as he figured out who this Koukai was.

The sun had just risen. He put his clothes on and walked outside. Splashing

his face with water from the barrel next to the door, he set off to build

more swords and work more on his secret project. He hadn't told anyone,

but he was creating armor made of leather for Kaito. It wasn't like armor

the samurai would later wear, but he felt it was more fitting for this period.

He learned how to work the leather with the same method as he had learned blacksmithing. He did use his abilities to place a few steel bands in between the layers of leather in the chest. He wasn't going to let his powers go unused; he had them for a reason.

Hana was going to leave in a few hours, so animals and items were being made ready for her stay, as this time, she would be staying until the child was born. As far as anyone noticed, Yuuto went about his regular routine. He spent a lot of time in the shop; in fact, it seemed he spent more time there since he met the Ainu. Their leader would come at times with a woman. The other workers assumed these meetings explained why he had changed since first visiting the Ainu. They believed a marriage of some sort was being arranged. The Ainu were viewed as primitives, little was known about their culture. They did agree the woman was attractive even though she wasn't Japanese. However, she seemed very stern and angry, which explained why she was unmarried, so they would let Yuuto keep her.

Judging by the sounds coming from the smithy, Yuuto was hard at work.. Today the woman came alone, and without looking at anyone, walked straight to the smithy. The hammering stopped, and then the removable wall of the smithy went up. Yuuto put the wall up so quickly that the men working nearby all looked at each other with a knowing smile. Though no words were exchanged, a few made hand motions illustrating their imaginings. The glances and looks disappeared when the sounds of steady hammering again echoed from the smithy. They were slightly disappointed, embarrassed, and perplexed. Why would a woman want to learn anything about blacksmithing? They exchanged a she must be crazy look, then one of the men voiced his idea that perhaps it was Yuuto who was crazy. All laughed and returned to their work, all thoughts of Yuuto and the woman forgotten.

*

Dan pressed the piece of wood, which was actually a play button for the hammering sounds for the others though to hear. He wouldn't do what the other men suspected, this woman was his sister in his Ainu family. Also, he could never be untrue to Sonya because of their unspeakable bond.

She was already trained in self-defense and combat. When she displayed greater skill than the cousin Rectify fought the first day he became family, he had to ask why he was so bad. She laughed. It turned out since the fire, he was always half drunk and had never been a great fighter to begin with. He tried to fight Sikanna at least once a month. While her fighting skills were excellent, she was unaccustomed to the nuances of espionage and counterintelligence. It was Dan's job to give her a crash course in surveillance.

He had many opportunities to do spy work in his time in special forces, and he loved it; it's something you either had a knack for or didn't. She was already well versed, but he knew he could teach her much more because she had the gift. He helped her improve her close-quarters combat abilities. She knew enough Japanese to get by. Dan wasn't sure if he would be able to work on her Japanese with her, but he found he could make himself speak in Japanese to her instead of Ainu with little mental effort. Primarily she was there to help protect Hana and listen for the name Koukai in the court and in the marketplace.

As far as Kaito, Hana, and their family knew, she was there as a symbol of the Ainu's willingness to serve Hana's family. That reminded Dan they probably needed to find another name for them since they were no longer accepted by the rest of their people. Hana had her ladies make his sister clothes appropriate for court. At Dan's request, they adapted them to allow for movement and hidden pockets.

From what he saw when on top of the mountain and his views from Hana's previous trip, he knew there was a wall around the family compound in the city, with space for the guards to patrol atop the wall. His plan was every day just after sunrise and before sunset, she was to drop a flower from the same place on the back wall to indicate all was well. She was to drop two if she heard the name Koukai and then report. If she did not drop a flower, they would take that as a sign of duress, and one of the Ainu men hidden inside the city would come to get the rest of the family and all of Kaito's men at the farm.

Dan knew he could have found Koukai and delivered the message himself, but felt it was important for the people involved to do as much as possible. Today was the final test for his sister. He was satisfied with her unarmed self-defense techniques but knew if it came to open unarmed combat in the field, she wouldn't last long as her enemies would likely be armed. On the other hand, give her a sword or staff, and she could last as long as anyone. As with the rest of her family, she was determined to do her part and give her life, if necessary, to maintain the family honor and protect their secrets from the world.

She was proficient enough in Japanese for anyone to believe she was a servant and enabled her to be more than just a bodyguard. Hana's two ladies were proficient with the blade, but they could not compare to his sister's s abilities in unarmed combat. Hopefully, when the time came, they could work together to protect Hana. Ready or not, it was time for her to go, and what was to happen, would happen. He still felt strange not knowing her name, but it was something the family held sacred, yet it felt weird to not know your sister's name, so he figured it couldn't hurt to ask. Both turned to leave the smithy, as his sister moved to open the door, Dan asked.

"Sister… I do not know all the ways of our family, but would it be proper for me to ask your name?"

Her cheeks reddened at his request.

"I am sorry, Brother, but it is not proper at this time for me to tell you my name. When the family order is restored, and Koukai is dead, I will tell you my name. One does not ask our name, but we tell our name when the time feels appropriate."

"Very well, Sister, I hope to hear your name soon, then I will tell you my true name." He felt like he should say more, but after an awkward silence, he finally blurted. "Well, it's time you are off. I have faith in you and know you will bring much honor to the family."

She gave a slight nod and reached for the door. Dan suddenly remembered he had left the hammering sounds playing. He quickly lunged for the button stopping the sounds just before she opened the door.

"Brother, sometimes you are very strange." Was what Dan heard as she exited, leaving the door open behind her.

With a laugh, he threw the piece of wood that served as his play button in the forge and started taking down the temporary walls around the smithy. Before he got started, he noticed a long branch he didn't recall seeing before. Suddenly he was struck with an idea. Recalling a European quarterstaff, he pictured a staff almost as tall as his Ainu sister with a sharp metal point that went in the ground. While retaining the image in his mind, he took the stick in hand, and it became what he pictured in his mind. It looked like a staff someone might use for support, but it could become a weapon in the right hands. Taking it, he quickly caught up with his sister and presented the staff to her.

"What is this?" She asked.

"It's a gift I made, but almost forgot to give you."

She took it in her hands, feeling its weight and balance, and recognized its dual purpose. For the first time since meeting her, she smiled.

"I shall keep this close Brother," she said as she patted his arm, her fingers brushing his hand as she hurriedly walked to the wagon.

Dan jogged back to the smithy to take the walls down, then hurried back to the house in time to wave to the ladies as they left for the city. Kaito walked over to him, reaching up to pat him on the shoulder.

"See Yuuto, I told you they didn't need any men to go with them. I trained those two women, and I know they will protect Hana and your friend."

"Yes, you are right. I was wrong to worry."

Sure Kaito had trained many people and trained the two women well. But Dan had trained people on nearly every continent; many women knew self-defense thanks to him. He almost hoped that someone would try something with his sister. He smiled at the thought of how surprised they would be if they tried anything with her.

"Yuuto, why are you smiling?" Kaito asked his friend.

"What?... a man can't find joy in the birth of a child?" Dan blurted out quickly.

"I guess you are right. But I'm going to miss Hana. Best we keep busy, why don't you show me what you've been working on in the smithy?"

"Alright, Follow me, friend..."

CHAPTER 10
KEEPING VIGIL

Hoyupu was one of ten assigned to watch for flowers being thrown over

the wall. He had been waiting for what felt like hours when he finally saw

one flower fall down the wall. It was sunrise, and all was well. There had

been no mention of Koukai. The four sentries covering the four sides of

the city reported back after sunset. Nothing was out of the ordinary other

than more merchants than usual. Yet, the number of merchants leaving was

at normal levels. Perhaps they were staying in anticipation of the festival

surrounding the coming birth of the city lord's child, or it was expected this

time of year, they weren't sure. The only thing they could do was wait and,

as always, be prepared for anything.

*

Hana awoke to the sound of birds singing outside her window. It was a

familiar sound, but in her time back in the city, she realized she had adapted to farm life and was almost surprised that she missed its sounds. Though it had not been long since the last visit, she found she still hadn't adjusted back to living in the city. Sitting up, she turned her head to avoid the sun and stretched her arms above her head. Gathering her wits about her, thoughts drifted to her last day in this room before she married Kaito.

She did not know him well but had always heard warriors were cold, cruel, and harsh, so she was scared when told by her father she was to marry the captain of his guard. She was surprised and scared, but she had always been drawn to Kaito's handsome face, his eyes looked so honest and honorable. Besides, she assumed they would be living in the family home, and he wouldn't dare hurt her in the presence of her family.

Her security was shattered when informed by her father he had given Kaito permission to be a farmer. She still remembered her father's admonition at her gasp. He reminded her of her duties to the family and how her actions reflected on the family's honor. Thinking back to those early days, she smiled. She had dreaded living on a farm and being a farmer's wife. Now she wanted nothing more than to get back to the farm and her Kaito, who was far different from any man she had ever met. He was a warrior because he hated war.

She wasn't sure why the Ainu woman was sent with her. She tried to tell her husband her two ladies were enough. He convinced her it would be good for the relationship between their people to have her and as a personal favor for Yuuto. She was pleasant enough, but never smiled and always seemed to be looking for danger or expecting something to happen, very improper for a lady of the court. It was probably because of the savage way she had been raised. However, there was one strange thing about her apparently, she loved flowers because, for the last three days, she had gone atop the wall with a flower both at sunrise and sunset and then returned without the flower. Perhaps it was part of their religion?

Her sister-in-law was doing well, so Hana had little to do other than stay by her side to visit and assist the physician on his daily visits. She had some exciting news herself after speaking privately with the physician, as he confirmed her suspicion that she was pregnant. She knew Kaito would be happy; she hadn't told anyone, so she could be the one to tell him. It weighed on his mind that there was no one to carry on the family name with his brothers gone. Even though he felt that pressure and obligation, he had never pushed her but waited until she was ready. Imagining his joy when he heard the news was the only thing keeping her sane during this time of waiting for her brother's baby. However, the growing excitement in the city for the upcoming festival around the birth helped a little. Most exciting was that a great merchant from the South would be coming to the family home in the afternoon to make preparations for the festival and the accompanying feast. Rising, she went to prepare for the day and her duties.

*

Dan wasn't exactly sure how many days it had been since Hana had gone to the city. He thought for sure she and Kaito were the ones he was here to help but wasn't as confident now. He tried asking Abel and offered many prayers asking for guidance or a hint as to who he was here to help, but Abel didn't show up this time. The only answer he got in his prayers was the admonition to be patient. Perhaps he was here to help his adopted Ainu mother but got even fewer answers about her. She was one person he felt he had helped, and assumedly that meant her family, but was there more, or was he done helping their family?

He didn't like downtime and never had; he always wanted to be busy. Otherwise, he would start thinking, his thoughts always going to Sonya. Of course, the situation right now wasn't any different than when he was alive. He was usually gone somewhere and couldn't message or visit as much as he would like. Even when he did, he was always careful not to say too much or reveal his feelings to make sure he didn't push her. The few times he expressed his love for her too much, she would quietly whisper, "I love you too," quickly followed by "I'm sorry I need to go." After the exchange, she would be unavailable for a time.

He honestly didn't know why he felt such a connection with her. Sure, they had become friends and dated before his mission; they had even dated after his mission while he was in the military. Well, he didn't know if you would say dated, it was more like they spent time together. Both felt content and complete when with the other. Dan had always wondered if perhaps the connection was somehow formed before they were born. Ever since his conversation with Abel and praying that day on the mountain, he hadn't checked on her. He was trying to wait until after completing this mission. But it wouldn't hurt to make a quick check on her; he was just about to open the space in his mind...

"Yuuto, where are you." Came the familiar voice of Kaito from his side.

"What?"

Kaito made a sweeping gesture with his arm at the river. "You were just sitting there, staring across the river."

"Oh... I was enjoying the day and then got to thinking about a woman from my past."

"Ah, you are not the first soldier I have known to have those same memories. Did someone close to you die?" Kaito asked with the tone of someone who understands loss.

The question took Dan by surprise. Kaito had no idea how right he was; someone did die. For whatever reason, his death hadn't really struck him until now, but... he was dead. Everything he'd hoped for and planned was done, yet there could still be a change. He was doing all of this for Sonya; he was going to change what happened to her, but then what would happen to him? Kaito made a slight noise that brought him back to the present.

"Yes... We were separated by death... I... I had so many plans. After I was done being a soldier, I was going to settle down with her and live happily ever after. But... ugh." He grabbed a pebble and threw it in the river. "Maybe it was only my dream, but I've never loved anyone else and can't imagine being able to love like that ever again."

A hand on Dan's shoulder made him look up from where he found himself sitting on the bank of a river. It was such an idyllic setting. The sun was shining, occasionally hiding behind one of the few clouds floating in the sky. There was tall grass interspersed with wildflowers amongst which bugs were buzzing, and birds were darting just above the grass. The sound of the wind blowing through the grass had a musical quality to it. Underneath it all was a voice aching to be heard. He heard the skittering of a brave squirrel running up a tree to his right, grabbing some treasure, and running back down to go somewhere farther away. It was the only tree within view of the bridge and tall enough to span the river should it fall. Sitting there, looking up at it, it seemed gigantic. *How long has that tree stood there?* he wondered *what things has it seen?* He looked back towards Kaito and started to open his mouth but didn't know what to say. Kaito perceived his friend was troubled.

Kaito followed Dan's gaze to the tree. "Ah, I see you have noticed our family tree; it has been something I have appreciated all my life. It marked my journey from the farm to the city, where I became a warrior and a man. It also commemorates when I left my life as a warrior to be a farmer and became complete with my wife next to me. Honestly, at the time, I wasn't sure if I could be a farmer, husband, or father. All my troubles seemed so big. Then, as I passed this tree, I was struck by a thought. As large and important as this tree seems to me, many trees in the forest are much older and larger, yet this one, when viewed alone, seems the most giant tree in existence."

"I know I'm speaking a great deal, but Hana was not the first woman I ever had feelings for. That first woman was like this tree when viewed alone, she was beyond compare, but when I truly saw her, I realized she would be nothing in the forest. Then I saw Hana, and when she became a woman, I saw that she would be the greatest and most majestic in the forest. It's like losing a piece of yourself to lose love, but I know even when it's lost, it can be found again, and you will find there are other trees in the forest that can make you forget the hurt. This holds true for all problems. They seem so big until you look in the forest."

Dan sat there nodding his head, Kaito's words made sense, but he just didn't understand the situation. There could never be anyone but Sonya. In a forest of Pine trees, she was a Sequoia. A sudden tug on the stick in his hand pulled him back to reality. So deep in thought, he forgot he was fishing. He jumped up and started pulling the fish towards him, he had never fished without a reel before, but if Tom Sawyer could do it, surely he could too.

Kaito and the other men had mocked him for attempting to catch a fish with a hook on a string attached to a pole. They saw it as futile when a net would bring in much more fish. It seemed all the mocking had been forgotten and was replaced by shouts of "pull it in" from Kaito and the other men that had been enjoying a day of no work. He grew tired of fighting with the fish and decided he would just follow the line and walk into the water to grab the fish. He got one foot in the water when suddenly he felt arms around his torso, pulling him back and throwing him to the ground, the fish flying over his head still on the line.

He was speechless, and all the men were silent. Judging by the looks on their faces, they were frightened of something. Finally, Dan said what was on his mind.

"Are you crazy? What are you doing!? Why would you do that"?

Kaito returned a look that insinuated Dan was the crazy person.

"Crazy? We weren't the ones stepping into the river?"

The confused look on Dan's face said more than words.

"Yuuto, how can a man be your age and not know what a Kappa is? Don't they have them where you're from?"

Again Dan was not able to hide the ignorance from his face.

"It is dangerous even to mention them this close to the water. They reside in rivers, and if you are unaware, they will pull you in and you will not be able to come back up!"

Using every ounce of self-control and decorum he possessed, Dan could barely keep from laughing out loud and making some kind of unkind remark. It could only be attributed to his current status because, in his mortal state, he would likely have stuck his foot in his mouth.

"Well..." Dan worked his tongue around in his mouth, searching for the right answer. "In my experience, I have never met a challenge or foe I could not defeat, so I welcome the challenge."

"Are you crazy!?" several of the men, including Kaito, said in unison as they quickly started gathering all their stuff. "It's time for us to get back to the farm. I want to start working on the new room in the house tomorrow, so we will need to start early. Besides, we have enough fish for tonight anyway, so we best be off."

Dan picked up his fishing pole and the rest of his fishing gear. He had heard of clearing the room before but never a whole river. *Thanks for all the preparation, Abel,* he thought to himself and swore he could hear laughter. He looked back toward the city one more time. He would guess that from the bridge to the town was 10 miles or 16 km, and the farm was probably a bit farther than that. Were someone at the top of the tree, they would see much of the surrounding area. He made a mental note to remember the tree for later.

The sun was close to going down by the time they got home. They had stopped midway to eat their fish, though none said anything; it was clear they wanted to get away from the river. Now home, he looked up to the sky, focusing on the first star he absent-mindedly thought, *Starlight, star bright, first star I see tonight, I wish I may, I wish I might have this wish I wish tonight. Please keep Sonya safe and happy.* He walked into Kaito's house, flopped down on his pallet, annoyed at another day wasted. He had never been very patient and loathed having to learn it now. Still, he would do whatever it took to finish this for Sonya.

*

Hoyupu, watching the wall for a flower to fall, was counting the days in his head and was sure it shouldn't have been his turn to watch for the sunset flower again. In fact, he was starting to wonder if the man they were looking for even existed, or if he did, perhaps he wasn't going to come here after all. Nevertheless, he would do whatever it was Grandmother and Uncle told him to do. After all, family and honor were more important than life or even boredom. The day before he had been watching the south entrance and saw many merchants enter the city, he thought for sure one group was suspicious. He followed them all the way to the gates of the palace, carefully watching them, but after speaking to someone at the gates, they set up tents nearby. A day later, it seemed all was well. He guessed he was wrong, and they were just traders. The shadows were growing long now as the sun was disappearing over the horizon. His aunt had never been so late dropping the flower, but he would give her until the last ray of the sun disappeared over the horizon. No flower fell.

He turned to the others and gave the signal that it was time to enact the plan. Four of them would go and gather the others, watching the entrances and infiltrate the palace. At the same time, he would run to the farm as he was the best runner in the family and report to the outsider... his now Uncle, Yuuto, or whatever his name was. From there, Yuuto would send another runner to notify the family to assemble at the farm.

He hurriedly made his way out the door, then slowed so as not to draw

attention, and kept to the sides of buildings in the shadows. He wanted to

run directly through the middle of town but didn't know how many

enemies were in the city or if the roads were watched. It took him 30

minutes just to get out of the city instead of the five it would have taken

had he run straight to the farm. He hoped it had been worth it. Finally, out

of the city and seeing the road was clear, he ran at the fastest pace he dared,

knowing the distance he would have to cover. He kept a steady pace until

reaching the bridge; once there, he looked back to see if anyone was behind

him and to take a breath. To his relief, he saw and heard no one; after a few

deep breaths, he turned to continue his run when he heard, no felt

something, he knew only because he had been around bows his entire life.

He leaped forward just as an arrow struck the bridge where he had been.

Hoyupu may not have been as smart as he was fast, but he knew when to

run.

This time he ran with no thought of conserving stamina, running for family

and honor. Should he die, he would die knowing he had given his all and

done his family proud. He just had to get the message to the farm. His legs

were burning, and his lungs aching… Over and over in his mind, he

repeated: *just a little more, just a little more, just a little more.* Hoyupu was seriously beginning to doubt if he would be able to make it out of this alive,

much less deliver his message. He couldn't recall ever running this fast, for

this long, running for practice and just to cover distance was far different

than running for your life. Trying to think of everything besides how tired

and sore he was, he couldn't help but berate himself for running out of fear

on the bridge. The pounding in his chest, the heavy burning breaths, and

the legs ready to collapse were forgotten when light from the farm appeared

in the distance. No longer worried about his life, he put his last ounce of

energy into his run. No matter what happened, his message would be

delivered, keeping his sacred honor intact.

*

Everyone at the farm was asleep, except for Dan. He just couldn't get

Sonya out of his mind. He took only a glimpse of her in his mind, watching

her longingly as she went throughout her day. There was some guilt because

he said he wouldn't watch her again, but nothing was happening, so what

could it hurt? Besides, he checked out his other family members for a few

seconds before he checked on her, so it wasn't just her. From what he could

see, she was happy with the volunteer work and her nursing studies. There

was nothing more beautiful than her smile. She was headed to meet a friend

for lunch. Suddenly in the back of his mind, from what he guessed was his

pesky conscience, was a push to focus on his current mission. Even though he knew it was ridiculous, he switched his view to Hana and those around

her.

*

The Ainu woman hadn't yet returned from her morning flower ritual. Hana

did her best not to be impatient with the woman and her ways, but she was

anxious to get her daily tasks done with the merchant due that afternoon.

Beyond seeing to her sister-in-law's needs, she had to see to the dealings

with the merchant for the celebration. She especially hoped she could finish

before the physician arrived.

Finally, the Ainu woman came back without her flower as usual, but Hana

hardly cared; she immediately beckoned for them to follow her. They

arrived only a few minutes before the physician. Hana thought she would

speak to the Ainu woman after this was all over, or if nothing else, ask her

name. However, it appeared her rush to get started was in vain. The

physician was worried and advised the room she was in was inadequate and

she needed to be moved to a quieter place, like Hana's room.

By the time they got her moved and settled, it was past time for the

merchant to arrive. It seemed nothing was going right today because the

merchant wasn't here yet either. Hana sent the Ainu woman to the gate to

watch for the merchant and then notify her when the merchant arrived.

*

The Ainu sister wondered if she should tell Hana her real name or give her a name to call her to avoid the awkwardness that accompanied their interactions. She decided she would take care of that when she returned, but for now, she was growing slightly concerned at the lateness of the merchant.

Exiting the palace doors, she saw a group of men, presumably the merchants, at the gates bringing many provisions. She was halfway to the gates when the two guards at the gate fell in unison. Then like a tidal wave, men began pouring into the palace, striking down all in their path. She turned and ran back to the palace screaming, "Enemy attack!" After passing the guards, she stopped screaming, climbed the stairs to Hana's room, and trying to remain calm while beginning to block the door. It didn't take long to explain her reasoning. After about 15 minutes, the faint sounds of battle stopped. They dared not check to see who won, but after 30 minutes, pounding on the door followed by demands to open gave all the answers they needed. She only hoped they could hold out until sunset and then hoped their rescuers would be successful.

*

Dan was immediately disgusted with himself upon viewing the scene. He saw Hana, her three ladies, her sister-in-law, who was in the beginning

stages of labor judging by her breathing. Two of the ladies were trying to

hold the door with his sister behind her staff, ready to strike. He saw a hand

get inside the door only to be pierced by the point of his sister's quarter-

staff followed by muffled swearing.

He jumped up, grabbing his sword as he ran to Kaito's room, shouting for

him to wake up. Hana was in trouble. After a few groggy moments, his

words soaked in, and Kaito jumped as high and fast as a track athlete in the

Olympics.

"Wha, how do you know something's wrong?" he sleepily asked,

fingers fumbling to fasten the new leather armor Dan had made for him.

"It's just a feeling I had. If I'm correct, a runner will be coming

from the city. I'll stand on the road to intercept him. I will bring him here to

rest, then head to the city. Do not follow until you are prepared, rouse the

men, make sure all are prepared for combat, signal the Ainu, and wait for

the Ainu to arrive before you follow."

Kaito almost said something about who was in charge;, though it was dark,

he did not need to see Yuuto's face to know by his words, there was no

need to question. The confidence in Yuuto's voice made him want to listen.

"I will do as you say, but I will follow as soon as the men and I are prepared whether the Ainu are here or not."

"Mmph" was Dan's only reply, receiving his expected answer.

Dan put all things out of his mind. He wasn't Yuuto or Dan; he was Rectify The Avenging Angel, a soldier preparing for battle. He was about to unleash a terror his enemy had never imagined. He put his sandals on, which he saw as boots, but the others saw as sandals and often teased him for taking so long to put them on. He donned the black clothes which he had set aside for night work. Last, he attached his sword in its scabbard to his waist and headed for the door to leave. Suddenly, he remembered the item Abel had given him when they spoke on the mountain. He had consigned himself to never having it again and so forgot he had Sonya's knife.

His hardened soldier façade cracked for a moment when he felt the familiar weight of the item in his hand. Memories came flooding back to him as he considered the thing in his hands. His memories went back to when he first became a Navy Seal when he was given this custom made knife by Sonya, even though the Navy gave him both an MK knife and a Ka-Bar. As far as knives go, there were better knives for his kind of work, and he had several in a box somewhere, but as far as he was concerned, this one knife was the greatest ever made.

Taking it out of the sheath, he held it up to the lantern, which cast only enough light to see its outline. He didn't need to see it to know exactly what it looked like, even down to the bladesmiths brand on the blade; it was an extension of his body. It had been with him on every mission or engagement he had ever participated in. In the confusion of his last assignment, it had been lost, his men unable to recover it. Apparently, Abel found it, and Dan was glad his men hadn't been able to so he could have it now.

With a 6 inch blade, no one would describe the knife as exceptionally large, especially when considering the knives used in movies like Rambo or Commando. It wouldn't win a knife competition with Crocodile Dundee, but he would take it over any of their's. Aside from being large and intimidating, those knives had one major drawback as a combat knife, in his opinion. They were shiny and reflected light, which was detrimental to stealth work.

Dan would never consider himself superstitious, as he thought things, like not changing socks, or wearing a specific shirt when your team was playing, were stupid. However, he never would have been caught going on a mission without his knife. Before any battle or engagement, he would find a place and time to get down on one knee and pray. Upon closing his prayer, and without even thinking, he would reach down and touch the knife at his waist to remember who he was fighting for. Attaching the knife to his belt opposite the sword, it felt right. Walking out the door, he felt the familiar S + D, which had been etched into the base by Sonya.

Before leaving his room, he said a prayer, felt his knife, and with this old friend at his waist, Rectify was finally ready to go to war. He couldn't recall ever being this excited to go on a mission in his life. Knowing he couldn't kill the redeemable was freedom at a level he had never felt.

CHAPTER 11
NIGHT FIGHT

Kaito was in the process of rousing the men and was surprisingly already wearing half of his armor, which was usually a long process. Dan tapped his shoulder before leaving and told him about the crates full of weapons in the smithy. He had gotten carried away a few times and made at least 15 new swords according to Kaito's design, as well as spears with a broad blade at the end. Kaito had asked him to only make a few of the swords, and no one should have been able to make that many in such a short time. Kaito took a brief pause as though he were going to ask a question, but dismissed it as other things were on his mind. Besides, he was glad his small number of men would be given a technological advantage.

Running from the farm's light to the road, Dan decided it was time to embrace Rectify. No sooner had he reached the road when a young man he guessed to be about 15 or 16 half ran, half stumbled into his arms. Between gasps, the boy was able to say "the words city... attack... Koukai..." before

Rectify had to catch him as he passed out. Quickly picking him up to cradle

him in his arms, he ran back to the house, depositing him on his bed.

He ran out of the house to the road, not planning to stop until he met an

enemy or reached the city. Running past the men this time, it was evident

that they were more earnest in their preparations, having seen the

messenger get carried in. Rectify soon put that out of his mind focusing his

senses only on the road and its surrounding area. He made sure to run in

the wagon wheel ruts of the road. Briefly considering the distance the Ainu

boy had run, he was very impressed at how difficult a run it must have

been. He noticed the boy's bloody feet as he laid him on his pallet, he had

run barefoot. He was happy to be wearing his boots. He almost pitied his

enemy if they were also running barefoot or in sandals. However, he wasn't

entirely sure about their footwear. Either way, he wouldn't be healing their

feet like he healed the boy's

His pondering came to a halt when he heard the sound of several feet

somewhere ahead of him. He didn't have much time before he ran into

them. They would surely be tired from their run, so this fight needed to be

fast. It was not the right place for his sword, so he drew his knife from his

waist, and sprinted toward the first enemy, grateful for the knowledge he

could only kill those deserving of death.

The first man heard Rectify moments before a knife struck him low in the neck, severing his windpipe. Rectify quickly retrieved his knife from the man's neck, instinctually seeking out his next target. The group of men had never seen anyone die so fast. Their fight or flight instinct kicked in, their first thought was to run and save their own life.

Knowing speed was his ally, Rectify ran like a linebacker at the other man who didn't have time to even turn around completely. Tucking his right shoulder down, he hit the man in the abdomen, sending him flying back about 6 feet, then closed his eyes as he sunk his knife into the man's heart. Remembering Abel's words that he could only kill those who were unredeemable, he guessed these two were not redeemable. If they were sent out for an assassination mission, they were very likely as wicked as Koukai. Stopping long enough to retrieve his knife, he heard the twang of two bows and quickly rolled to the side just before two arrows struck the corpse he had tackled.

The bowmen were about 10 paces away, and had it not been for Rectify's enhanced reflexes, he would have been hit. The two men were stunned he managed to slip their arrows and paused long enough to give Rectify time to rip the helmet off the dead man and throw it at the nearest bowman. It did no damage, but natural human reactions made him drop his bow to block the object coming towards his head. The man successfully stopped the helmet, knocking it into his comrade's bow, sending his next shot at the

charging Rectify wide. Rectify drew his sword and was on his next assailant

in only a few seconds. Slicing upward, the man instantly lost his life. The

last man, his bow now discarded on the ground, drew a short sword and

lunged at Rectify, but his thrust was easily parried. Rectify with his longer

blade knew that in close fighting, the shorter blade had the advantage,

leaped backward. Every attempt made to close the gap by his opponent was

met with a perfect block or parry. Despite all his efforts, he was never able

to close the distance.

Despite all his attempts to be a no-nonsense avenging fighting machine as

Rectify, Dan grew tired of his opponent's attempts to kill him. The man was

visibly worn, and after yet another unsuccessful thrust, he paused to catch

his breath. Once again, reflecting on one of his conversations with Abel, he

didn't want to kill this man who was no longer a threat. Among his various

thoughts was. *Perhaps this is one of the men I can't kill because he is still redeemable?*

Dan viewed his clearly exhausted opponent and couldn't bring himself to

do anything other than spare him.

The tired assassin looked up in surprise when he heard the sound of that

wicked curved blade returning to its scabbard. He was unaccustomed to the

concept of mercy, knowing only weakness or strength. He knew the man he

fought was a skilled swordsman, but he must be weak to yield an advantage like this.

"You have fought well and honorably; therefore, I will not kill you and release you to return to where you will."

Dan turned and was halfway through his first step away, when suddenly to his mind came the image of the man stabbing him in the back. His first thought was it was nerves. The second thought had him grasping his knife and quickly turning left, just as to his side a blade thrust past him to his right, perfectly aligned with where his kidney had just been. With the same speed as Dan had turned, he thrust the blade upwards, it disappearing as it met the underside of his opponent's jaw.

Looking down at his former opponent, he suddenly realized he was bleeding on his side, where the blade from the dead man had drawn blood. *But I'm Rectify. How could he make me bleed?* Abels's voice sounded in his head.

"Because you didn't fight him as Rectify, you fought him as Dan Campbell. No earthly being can hurt Rectify. Need I say more?"

He had to decide whether he was Dan Campbell, the soldier, a man distracted by things he couldn't change, and who longed for Sonya, or was he Rectify? The same Rectify, who was somehow fighting for the whole world and had the assurance that he would receive everything he had ever dreamed of at the end of his mission.

The answer was simple. Rectify thought of the screens in his mind and removed all not related to the task at hand. Retrieving his knife, he wiped the blade and began to run at his inhuman speed for the city. A few miles away from the bridge, he could see bright flames reaching into the night sky made dark by a cloud-covered moon, where the bridge should have been. In the time it took him to reach the bridge, the flames had disappeared, having been put out by the river and running out of fuel to burn.

This would pose no problem for Rectify as he could jump over the river. No enemies were in sight, evidently thinking the missing bridge would cause a delay in any retaliatory attacks. Summoning all his strength and focusing on the opposite bank, he leaped and amazed himself at the inhuman feat he had just accomplished. He was a few steps into his continuing run when he suddenly remembered those following him had a fear of the Kappa. Ensuring that none but Kaito would cross because nothing could stop Kaito from reaching his Hana. However, he would need more than just one man besides himself to make the following events seem remotely humanly possible.

Reluctantly, Rectify jumped back across the river. It wasn't as impressive this time, as it was one of many steps towards understanding he was Rectify. Surveying his surroundings and lack of observers, he remembered Abel's message that he had permission to do anything to accomplish his task. At first, he thought to do as Moses or Joshua in the bible and part the water for the other men to cross. That was quickly crossed off his list as it definitely wasn't a human thing to do. These men had never heard of the parting of the Red Sea or Jordan River. They would surely be too scared to cross. His second thought was to touch the bridge and make it repair itself, but he also knew that wasn't the right thing.

Considering the limited time Hana and the other ladies had before the enemy breached the room, Rectify paced as he was frantically trying to get an idea. It would be really stupid if everything was ruined because he couldn't figure out how to make a way for the other men to cross the river. A sudden gust of wind arose from behind him, almost deafening him with the rustle of branches and foliage from the tree by the river Kaito had shown him. Just as quickly as the gust of wind had appeared, it stopped, but he got the message whoever was trying to send him.

Walking to the tree, he scanned up and down. It was undoubtedly tall and straight enough to span the whole river. It looked wide enough for someone to be able to walk across without much trouble. Just to get an idea of what he was dealing with, Rectify reached his arms around the tree, his cheek turned flat against the trunk and found his fingers could not touch. Once he was sure the tree was tall and wide enough to span the river and get the men across, he wasn't sure how to go about chopping it down. He had no ax nor the time to chop it down properly. For a brief moment, he wondered if with his accentuated strength, he would be able to kick or punch it hard enough to knock it over.

He regretted having to kill a tree that was special like this one, both for it's sentimental value and also because it was healthy, but it would fulfill a purpose. Putting his hand on the tree, he didn't know why, but he felt compelled to apologize to the tree for his next act. Conscience satisfied, he planted his feet, rared his arm back, then summoning all his strength, punched the tree, and heard a crack. The tree shook, and tiny pine needles fell all around, but it didn't budge. Rectify was shocked to feel excruciating pain in his hand. Looking down at his hand, he was astonished. The tree didn't break; his hand did, not just a finger or two, but every finger and some of the bones in his hand. His shock at breaking his hand was quickly replaced with amazement when he watched his hand return to normal and stop hurting almost instantaneously.

His fast healing was another reminder he wasn't Dan Campbell anymore. He was Rectify, who had not only the power but the permission to do what he deemed was right. Sheer brute force obviously wasn't the answer, but he had already wasted too much time trying to figure out how to make a way for the other men to get across. Again placing hands on the tree, he spoke to the tree with his mind. *I do not want you to die, but I command you to keep as many roots in the ground as you can and fall across the river.* Even before opening

his eyes, he felt the tree move. Upon opening them, he was greeted by the

sight of the tree moving. He jumped back as roots started coming through

the ground, and in seconds felt the earth shake when the tree landed.

Having wasted enough time, he ran across the tree to the city, only stopping

at the gates of the royal family's home.

CHAPTER 12
RECTIFY VISITS

Above the gate stood two men shadowed by the light of torches, who

challenged Rectify.

"Who goes there?" called out one of the guards.

"I come on behalf of my master Kaito. I am here for his wife,

Hana, those who accompany her and all her family."

The words were not spoken as a servant, but with all the confidence he had

seen every hero speak with. He expected them to laugh him to scorn as he

was only one man, but instead, there were a few shouts and some

mumbling. Five minutes later, another voice called down. It sounded like

someones' boss.

"Does Kaito still live? And who are you to approach this fortress?"

"Kaito is quite alive. Next time send more men. He is on his way, but I'm here to offer you a chance. Surrender this fortress, leave its

occupants inside, and you will all live." This time despite the authority of his

words, they were met with laughter.

"Let me in that I may speak to the honorless coward Koukai." He

couldn't help but smile, knowing how angry his words just made someone.

The man on the gate spluttered as he tried to speak. "You, you dare

speak the name of my Lord, you filth! I will rip out your tongue and feed it

to the dogs.- -"

"Ha, you can try, but first, you will hear my message, and I know

your master is listening, so you will be silent that he may hear my words.

For now, I give you permission to call me Yuuto; as I said, I am here to

offer peace. Leave, and you will all keep your lives. Stay, and all will die!"

He kept his voice calm. A real soldier knows the infinite power of

controlled anger.

A few moments later, the man at the top of the gate spoke as though

Rectify were the stupidest man on earth.

"My Lord says the words of a fool are of little worth, but he will

always allow a brave fool to speak his last." The gates opened. Behind them,

the pathway to the family home was lined on both sides with soldiers, fully

dressed for battle. Halfway between the entrance and the house were five steps. At the top of the steps, hands on hips, dressed in all his battle glory stood a man who must've been Koukai.

In a condescending tone, the man spoke. "Welcome to my city, fool. I see you are no fool in your intelligence, but only a fool in who you serve. You are wasting your life for a farmer and his possessions. I see you are a warrior. Soon my father and I will own all this land, and your skills would be of benefit to me, work for me, and you will be rewarded. I will give you riches and land."

Suddenly all politeness left his voice. "Fight me, and you will die!"

Dan was preparing an epic response and trying to decide between a chuckle or a belly laugh when, Koukai stopped talking.

Then Koukai messed everything up. Returning to his fake polite voice. "Bring me the head of Kaito, and I will not only give you land, but I will also give you the first turn with his wife and those with her, who I assure will bring you joy." He said with a sneer barely evident in the firelight.

Rectify could not answer for several moments; all thoughts of laughter replaced by hatred. His controlled anger had nearly been unleashed, but he knew he had to wait for Kaito and his men.

"I would sooner die a thousand deaths than serve scum like you. I will kill every man here if a finger so much as touches one strand of hair on any woman in this fortress."

*

Hana and everyone else in the room had managed to keep the door from being forced opened but knew it wouldn't stay closed much longer. The enemy had managed to break through it in many places. Then suddenly, the enemy stopped and left the door. All were braced for a new attack, but none came. They dared not open the door but listened intently and heard two people speaking. They were not sure what they heard but were confident they heard Kaito and Yuuto's names, which filled them with hope. During all the struggles, the baby had been born; it was a boy and heir, if any of them survived the night, but now there was hope. All was quiet until the night thundered with the sound of laughter. Two of the Ainu men who had gone out to investigate after the enemy left returned, and all feelings of safety diminished with the forlorn looks on their faces.

*

Koukai and all his men burst out in laughter. It took Koukai several breaths to stop laughing so he could speak.

"Go get your master, and return. I promise you will have my

answer on your return."

There's always a time to fight and a time to wait. In special forces training, you learn to make plans and then assume that the plan will change, and at some point, you will have to adapt. If all is going as planned, go with it. Rectify remembered one of his instructors at Annapolis, telling that planning was simple in the first Gulf War. All they had to do was think of the worst plan possible, and that was precisely what Saddam Hussein did. So far, despite all of Koukai's pride and disposition, he was proving to be the same caliber of tactician.

"Very well... Koukai." Rectify deliberately avoiding the lord part and getting his desired reaction when he saw a momentary twitch in the corner of Koukai's mouth. Koukai was clearly trying to assert his dominance and show that a common man's words meant nothing to him.

Rectify was halfway to the gate when he heard Koukai.

"If you and your master do not return or enter those gates with anyone besides yourselves, I promise your precious women will be publicly shamed and enslaved."

Rectify took a few more steps, checked his anger, then turned around.

"Oh, I promise you, I will return, and my sword will not be put away until you and all those who stay and fight beside you die."

That said, he untied the scabbard from his belt, drew his sword, and threw the scabbard into the darkness. He then turned around and walked out the gates, not stopping until he heard the gates being barred shut. He stepped around the side of a building and thought that he wanted his clothes to change from dark to white. He walked back onto the street all in white and knew he would be difficult for anyone to miss in the dark because when he returned to face Koukai, he wanted an example made.

*

Several hours later, Kaito, the men from the farm, and the Ainu arrived. It was about three in the morning, and the moon shone brightly, making Rectify almost glow in the white clothes he was wearing. He could see confusion and curiosity on the men's faces as they looked at him. Kaito momentarily paused, looking at Rectify as though he saw a different person than he had come to befriend over the past few months.

"Yuuto?" Kaito paused, trying to formulate his words. "How did you dispatch those four men on the road, cross the river and arrive so fast?"

Rectify had forgotten some of his exploits would be hard to explain, and he hadn't taken time to formulate an answer. The last several hours, he had spent pondering his life, the things that had brought him here, and where they could possibly go after this. He had almost turned his mind to Sonya but stayed strong and remembered what he was here for. With the expectant Kaito looking at him for an answer, he said the first thing that came to his mind.

"Luck! They weren't expecting a single opponent, and I caught them off guard. If it had been anyone else, the results would've been the same. As to the tree across the river, I was just as surprised as you. Just before I arrived at the river, there was a great gust of wind. Did you not feel it also?"

Kaito's eyes narrowed as he considered the words of his friend.

In a very unbelieving tone, Kaito nodded agreement.

"Yes, luck can be very beneficial, and I too felt the wind, but that tree has stood for many years and weathered many storms. How could this one gust of wind blow it over?"

Rectify shrugged his shoulders.

"Who can say? The gods must be on our side. Now we must be about business."

"Yes, exactly, we will attack the gates immediately, and I will see that all enemies in this fortress die."

Rectify reached out to calm his friend, related the events with Koukai, and assured Kaito all would be well. They would be able to get the women out with no bloodshed. The 20 or 30 men stayed about 100 yards from the gates, with strict orders to not approach until the gates opened. With orders given, Rectify and Kaito approached the gate, both men cautious but hopeful all would be resolved. Kaito's head was filled with thoughts of saving his beloved and then he would siege the fortress at the side of his Lord and brother in law. Rectify was sure this would be a long night. He would have to fight every man and of course, he would win.

CHAPTER 13
THE STUFF OF LEGENDS

The gates swung open, and both men walked forward, uncaring of the six

men by the gate behind them. They continued when suddenly Kaito

shouted out in pain. Rectify turned in time to see him on the ground, a

spear in the back of his thigh. Two more held against his neck, with the

other three pointed at Rectify. Enraged by the honorless treachery, Rectify

raised his blade, his legs tensed, preparing to leap onto the enemy, only

stopping at the voice of Koukai.

"Yuuto, perhaps I was wrong, and you are a fool. I must warn you

no common man has ever dared refuse me. I told you Kaito could enter

with you, but I told you to bring me his head. Make one move, and he dies,

as well as all your men outside the gates."

Rectify chided himself for trusting his enemy. But everything he knew

about Japanese culture made him think even Koukai was incapable of going against honor. He understood being fooled about Kaito, but how could he have been fooled concerning the men outside? He was just with them, and surely, he would have sensed a nearby enemy. He smiled, knowing his enemy could not bluff him, but he couldn't let Koukai know that.

"First, Koukai, you weak insect, I am no common man, as you will soon witness."

Koukai's mouth closed into a tight, barely controlled rage.

"Second, your act of treachery against Kaito will not go unpunished, and I know you lie about my men outside the gates."

Rectify wanted to kill the spearmen, so he decided to challenge the enemy to open the gates. Between the time the men at the gate questioned the order and Koukai lied, he would use his speed to strike them all down and heal Kaito. Koukai could only respond with

"You insignificant fool, how dare you speak to me in such a manner. It is you who are mistaken. You are helpless with no hope of rescue. Surrender, and you may yet live. I have always wanted a eunuch servant. Perhaps you can be the first."

"Very well honorless Koukai, I will expose yet another lie, go ahead and open the gates. Show me my captured men."

Rectify was un-prepared for Koukai to accept his challenge. With a snap of his fingers, the spearmen opened the gate, and Rectify was shocked to see his men surrounded by armed soldiers. However, he saw only the men from the farm, the Ainu were gone, but he knew he must not reveal their absence.

"What, how can this be?" Rectify gasped.

Koukai laughed. "You fool! Did you truly think you and your men stood any chance against me? Soon all this land will be mine, for the gods are on my side. The only chance Kaito and your men have is for you to do as you promised and fight us all. Perhaps when you are dead, I will allow those who join me to live. The others, including your precious women, will see you in the shadowlands of Yomi-no-Kuni."

Somehow Rectify knew this was hell in the Shinto religion. At least now, he had a vague idea this was before Buddhism had grown in Japan. It was also apparent he was going to get his chance to make this a memorable fight. Still, he was filled with caution because, somehow, the enemy's actions had been blocked from his knowledge. As far as he knew, that was impossible.

Rectify tried to sound joyful, "Of course I will fight! Unlike you, I am a man of my word, and I will be pleased to kill you and all your men. First, will you allow me to attend to Kaito and help him outside the gates, where the other men can help him?"

Koukai motioned that he could go outside, but made it clear it didn't
matter.

"You only delay the inevitable. You will both die this night, so it
matters not. But perhaps he will live long enough to watch your dear
women suffer ignominious deaths. When you are ready to die, return to the
palace."

Koukai returned to the palace with the deepest of smirks as he imagined the
pitiful sight of Rectify walking out the gates, one arm around Kaito, and the
other his naked blade. He could see himself as the great warlord and
emperor he was destined to be, for he was favored by the gods. All the
world would know his name and fear the mention of him and the curved
blade he would soon be taking from the foolish Yuuto.

All but two of the six spearmen followed their master; the other two stood
next to the open gate.

After Koukai turned, Rectify rushed to his friend. Kaito had lost quite a bit
of blood, luckily the spear was partially stopped by the armor Rectify made,
and it missed major arteries. Without conscious thought, he placed his hand
over the wound and thinking the words healed it. Kaito turned his face to
Rectify in surprise when he felt the heat in his leg, and then all pain

vanished. Unbeknownst to Rectify, who thought he had done an excellent job of hiding his abilities, Kaito had noticed.

From the very first day, it seemed strange that right, when he needed somebody, Yuuto arrived, and though he brushed it off, he knew no one could have done that much smithing in one night. His suspicions had continued to grow, and many times he thought to ask his friend but had always talked himself out of it. Watching Yuuto heal his leg, he could no longer restrain himself.

"Yuuto, who are you? Are you Kami?"

Rectify was taken aback because he didn't recognize the word Kami. Usually, he was able to automatically translate words. Reaching out, he sensed what Kaito was thinking and discovered that Kami were like gods or protectors to Kaito. What surprised Rectify the most was that Kaito thought he was some hero from the past sent to help him. Kaito wasn't wrong. In fact, Rectify smiled at the truthfulness of this thought, as he was a fallen warrior and some kind of protector angel, so he couldn't say no.

Looking at Kaito, all he could do was smile, "Perhaps I am, if I walk back out these gates, maybe I am, but right now we have some business to attend to. I need you to act like you are still hurt, and if you see men run out the gates, I need you and the other men to charge forward.

No matter what!"

Kaito gave the slightest nod of acknowledgment. Feigning support from Rectify, he hobbled through the gate to his men.

"Save Koukai for me," Kaito whispered.

"I will leave Koukai for you. You have my word, and after I will tell you who I really am."

Had it been any other man, Kaito would've thought it an empty boast. Though he still thought it impossible, he knew if any man or whatever Yuuto was could do it, it was him.

Upon handing Kaito to their men, Rectify tried to feel where the Ainu had gone as he returned to the gates, but could find no trace. Surely they wouldn't have abandoned him? No, of course not! They would show up at some point. Entering the gates, he cleared his mind of nonessential thoughts, only vaguely aware of the gates closing behind him.

*

Hana watched the events unfolding with dread, through a crack in the window shutter of her room. Her heart fluttered in her throat when she saw Kaito, and her feelings soared knowing that surely now they would all be freed and somehow things would be set right. Instantly everything

195

plummeted to the bottom of a high cliff when she saw the spearmen

casually walk up behind her husband and stab him in the back of the thigh.

She was fully prepared to see her love be killed. She yelped with joy when

the unbelievably fast reflexes of Yuuto ensured that could not happen. She

couldn't hear words or see Kaito after he hit the ground. She was beyond

relieved when she saw he and Yuuto exit the gates. At least perhaps Kaito

would live and avenge them.

The Ainu woman had joined her at the shutter, and Hana could swear she

heard the other's heartbeat hasten when Yuuto returned. Hana softly placed

her hand on the other woman's arm to comfort her for what she was about

to see. Both women knew they were about to see their only hope cut down

and have their fates sealed. Hana thought and hoped that perhaps her

husband was correct.

Kaito had the idea that Yuuto was no mortal man, and in fact, was a Kami

sent here to aid or protect them. Hana, too, had inklings he was no ordinary

man, and she had to admit he had skills. She wanted to believe he was right,

and Yuuto was about to save them all, but she just couldn't convince her

mind. In his unmistakable white clothing, they watched Yuuto walk up the

five steps in the center of the fire lit courtyard. It looked to be about an

hour before sunrise. The fire reflecting off his sword seemed to match the

fire in his walk; he was prepared for this to be his last battle. The enemy were arrayed before him in a three-sided square with the open side towards him. He stopped where the fourth line of the square should have been. This time, all in the room could hear his words as he shouted for all to hear.

"Koukai, I told you I would return, and if any treachery occurred, I would kill you and all your men who would not surrender. Now you have forced my hand, and you will all die! Rest assured; you will be last. You will watch all of your men and plans disintegrate in front of you, and then Kaito will have the honor of taking your head."

The soldiers stood at attention, not making a sound, in preparation for their Lord to speak.

"Oh my!" Koukai exclaimed with over-exaggeration. "You sound so frightening. How will my men and I have a chance against a cripple and a fool?"

Directing his arm towards his men. "I have 150 of the greatest soldiers to ever live, and I have gods on my side, but," shaking his head, "this is only the beginning. So indeed, I am quite afraid. Afraid your blood will stain the ground and one of my men will step in it. If you insist on dying, then come forward, and die like a man!"

Taking a cord from behind him, Rectify tied his hand around the sword hilt, then took it in both hands and looked around at each man, ending his gaze at Koukai.

" I think you'll find I'm more of a challenge than you think. I say

again, I am not who you think I am."

Hana's breath caught in the back of her throat. Was Kaito right? Was Yuuto

or whoever he was indeed here as their protector? From what she could

see, he showed no fear whatsoever, obviously not the reaction Koukai

expected.

Koukai took the bait

"Then tell me, fool, what shall I call you?"

Hana nearly fainted and wanted to shout out to Yuuto, but she couldn't

take a breath, much less get a word out.

*

Rectify knew he was about to test his abilities for the first time, but what

was the worst that could happen? If he died, he could just come back like

last time. It was hard to keep his excitement in check. He was about to play

out a scenario that action movies could only dream of, *one man against 150.*

Ha, eat your heart out, Arnold. But he had a job to do and pulled himself back

out of his head. His moment of contemplation over, he was ready to tell all

the name for which they should tremble.

"My name is not, Yuuto I am- -"

Rectify was cut off by a deep voice from behind him.

"Rectify!" the voice bellowed.

Immediately Koukai and all his men fell to one knee, bowing their heads. Rectify wasn't sure what to do with himself. He slowly turned and was shocked at the sight before him. It was a man at least 7 ½ feet tall and seemingly half as wide. He wore iron scale armor wielding a hammer nearly as tall as Rectify with a head larger than his. Rectify didn't know how he knew, but he knew this was no man. But how? There was no such thing as monsters, yet this thing didn't seem human.

On first look, it appeared human, but when looking at this thing and genuinely trying to see what it was, it clearly wasn't. It's skin had a greenish tint with a damp sheen, and the face slowly became more animalistic. It's eyes were uncomfortably spaced; instead of a nose, it had a broad sharp, what could only be described as a beak, not hard like a bird's beak but softer, and it also formed it's mouth. A person might have been tempted to think it looked like a Ninja Turtle. But, where their features were round and friendly, this thing's face had sharp ridges and looked evil. It's face looked like the blending of a human, turtle, and vulture. It was hard to gauge it's body because it was covered in armor, but it certainly was wide enough to have a shell.

Rectify finally managed to get over the shock of having his epic reveal interrupted and regained composure enough to speak.

"How, how do you know my name, and who... what are you?"

The thing tossed its hammer from one slightly webbed hand to the other as though it was a feather duster, and cocked his head to one side, looking directly at Rectify as though he was looking inside him.

"Come now Rectify, is that any way to speak to your brother?"

Rectify knew this was no brother of his and knew there was no way anything should know his real name. *What in the! What's going on?*

His thoughts were interrupted by the thing in front of him.

"Why, Rectify? You don't remember me, do you?" It's mouth beak raised up in a creepy imitation of a smile. "You don't remember your treachery and betrayal. We have watched and waited long for you. Never did I dream I would be the one to kill you."

Rectify was thoroughly confused. Who did he betray and what, who was this thing talking about?

"I have no idea who you are, and to my knowledge, I've never betrayed anyone. I am Rectify, and I'm here to right wrongs Stand in my way, and you will die just like the rest. No mortal being or weapon can kill me."

The giant before him let loose a deep hollow laugh that seemed to shake the sky.

"I think you'll find I am no mortal, and I can kill you, for that is the pact. When I capture you, we can kill all of you. Don't worry, before we kill you, you'll get to watch them all die, especially your favorites, and how we will relish killing the one you love most! Over the eons, we will teach you a new definition of pain and torture, as you beg to die."

What in the heck is going on? What pact, what does it mean by all of you, and how does it know about Sonya? Abel, this would be an excellent time for you to pop in my head and help me understand this.

Abel's voice sounded in his head. "I didn't know he was here. I meant to prepare you, but not like this. This is really not the time to explain, and there's a lot I can't tell you right now. But remember when I told you there were things you won't remember until you are dead, dead? Well, let's just say you made a lot of beings eternally angry before you were born on earth, and they have been waiting for their revenge for a long time. These guys hate you with a hatred beyond anything you can fathom. You hated Aco.

Multiply that by 100, and you will get an idea of their hatred."

Rectify gulped. *Thanks a lot, and wow, that's a lot of hate. But this thing can't kill me, right? What's this pact he's talking about, and what does he mean by all of you?*

"Look, I'm sorry it happened this way, but I'll make it all clear at some point, but yeah, he can kill you, and if you die... Well, let's just say the mission of Rectify is over, and everything and everyone you love is lost. Long ago, before you became mortal, you were forced to make a pact with an enemy, that they could not recognize you in life and would not know when you were born, but they would know when those who helped you were born. They could not harm them directly unless they captured you first. I'm not allowed to tell you who the others are, but you care a great deal about them."

So when he says they will kill the one I love most, this means they would be able to kill Sonya.

The response from Abel didn't come for a few seconds.

"Yes, he can kill all those closest to you, so they can kill Sonya if you fail."

Well, then I guess I just won't lose. Am I still able to heal quickly?

"Yes, just not as quickly as you've experienced so far. His kind clouds your abilities, so don't get hurt, or you could die."

Oh great, his kind. You mean there's more?

"Not now. You don't have much more time. Good luck!"

Yeah, good luck, thanks! Rectify thought sarcastically

His inner monologue was cut short when a gigantic hammer slammed into his left bicep. Arm broken, he went flying into a rank of men, knocking them down like bowling pins. Had the sword not been tied to his hand, it would've gone flying too. He didn't have time to contemplate the pain or the fact that his left arm was flopping across his chest and back with every movement. Quickly getting to his haunches, he immediately rolled right to avoid a downward swing of the massive hammer that would've pulverized anything it hit. He was able to get back to his feet and uselessly slice at the side of the thing while it picked up the hammer for another swing. He tried to bring his hand up to the hilt to hold it two-handed, but his left arm was still useless, but it was slightly itching, which must've been a good sign.

Thank you so much for the warning Abel! Don't get hurt, or you could die. You couldn't have said that a little earlier? Like before I started.

But he didn't give Abel time to respond.

The hammer back in it's hands, the thing came at him again, but Rectify was able to move just a little bit faster. Not fast enough that he could let his guard down. The thing came at him again, both hands holding the hammer in the middle. His enemy had a significant reach advantage, at the same time, he would be at a disadvantage up close. Rectify charged in aiming his sword in a downward killing slice at his opponent's neck. Only the giant quickly blocked it with his hammer then thumped the butt of the hammer into the side of Rectify's head. The metal pommel missed, but the wooden shaft connected, so it didn't knock him out, but he kept seeing weird spots in his right eye. Leaping back, he gave himself 10 feet of space.

Come on, man, get your head in the game! You're a freaking Navy Seal, Delta Force Operative, Doak Walker Award winner, and an Angel. You are Rectify! The fact that you got a whole bunch of people ticked off at you from before you can remember says they are still afraid of you, so you have been a bad dude your entire existence. So think! What does this guy expect you to do?

And then he had it. The enemy again charged towards him. The hammer swung at his ribs with such force that had it connected, his heart would've been crushed. The thing expected Rectify to either stand his ground or attack but wasn't prepared for what Rectify did next. Rectify turned and ran towards the gate, clearing the five steps in the middle of the courtyard by 15 feet with one leap. His opponent just standing there.

"What is this game you play, Rectify? The Rectify I knew would never run. Has your experience with mortality made you so weak?"

"Not weak, just a little smarter, but then it doesn't take much to outsmart you. What is your name anyway? I always like to know who I'm about to kill."

"Scum! Don't speak to me of names. Because of you, I have no name, but you may call my brothers and me, Kappa."

Hmm. Rectify thought. *I'm going to have to ask Abel how and why they don't have names because of me?*

"You're kidding. Kappa, like the silly things people think, are in the water?"

The Kappa, or whatever he was, was insulted.

"We have been relegated to living in the water since before man was on the earth. We are the monsters all people fear, and through their fear, we have been gaining strength over the eons until we were ready to take our place as the gods of the Earth. You, Rectify, will have the fortune of seeing those you once thought your lesser destroy you and all that you hold precious!"

Rectify, and the Kappa continued fighting. Rectify would run, stop, and wait for the Kappa to come to him and then run again. The Kappa was

clearly getting angry.

"You coward, stop running!" the thing shouted, slightly winded.

"Why should I do that? When you are stupidly beating yourself."

Rectify answered playfully and not short of breath. "Hey, I'm going to do

you a favor and give you a name. I dub thee Yertle." The thing clearly

wasn't expecting that and stopped.

"Wh- what?" the Kappa asked breathlessly

"Ha, trust me, it's funny, but maybe you'll get it someday well, not

you because you are about to die, but someone will get it." Rectify thought

it funny.

Come on, Abel, at least tell me you got it.

Abel's voice sounded in his head. "Yeah, I get it, but I really don't think this

is the time for bad jokes. You are just making him mad."

Rectify smiled. *Exactly, and my jokes aren't bad… they are just too intellectual for*

some people.

He was pulled back to the present when Yertle again spoke.

"You are a fool to mock me! I'll destroy you!"

"Aww, did I make poor little Yertle mad? Maybe you need a nap?

The Kappa was too angry to admit it, but he was growing worried because he could tell he was starting to get tired, and Rectify wasn't. *He may not remember the way he was before, but he's just as cocky. But there's no way he's as good as he was. He will slip up, and when he does, I will destroy him and punish him as he watches all those he protects cease to exist because of his failure.*

Rectify hoped the Kappa was genuinely getting tired and not just pretending to lull him into a false sense of security. He was pretty ticked at Abel for not preparing him, but was trying to keep that out of his mind because he needed to focus on the fight. He knew there was something different about this fight, and this thing he was fighting, and to get any answers, he had to survive the battle. When he started all this, he was confident nothing could kill him permanently. Still, somehow, he had the idea this thing really could kill him, possibly to the point of non-existence. He continually probed it's mind for any clues to the past and what it was feeling. He wasn't sure but thought he was starting to make progress.

It was evident this thing hated him, and it was a deep hatred beyond anything Rectify could comprehend. He truly believed it was billions of years worth of hate.

Once more, the Kappa lunged at him with inhuman ability, but again

Rectify dodged. It felt like he had been fighting for hours with no progress. In his probing's, he had to smile when coming across the thought that he was just as cocky as before. *At least I'm consistent* echoed in his mind. *I wonder what Koukai and his men are doing.* Rectify was amazed. Though it seemed they had been fighting for hours, Koukai and his men had barely moved, and it was still dark. *What is this thing if the rest of the world stops while we fight? What is…*

All thought vanished from Rectify's mind when a giant square of iron slammed into his chest. He not only felt but heard the sound of his ribs cracking. He briefly felt his feet lift from the ground before he slammed into the wall and slid down it, losing consciousness for about five seconds. Opening his eyes, the Kappa was now standing above him, and behind him, all of Koukai's men chanted, "Kappa!"

"Heh, you're nothing like you used to be. The boss is going to reward me big time for this. We have cursed you all these millennia and longed for a day when we could seek our vengeance. I've dreamed of this moment, but never thought I would actually be the one that got to destroy you and all you hold dear." He took a step back to give him room to bring his mighty hammer down through the top of Rectify's skull, but stopped.

"I almost wish I was fighting the old Rectify, they always said you were powerful, but I knew I could take you. Oh well, we don't always get what we want."

With that, he hefted the hammer above his shoulder and swung down. Rectify had been trying to reach for his sword, but when he hit the wall, the cord holding it slipped, and he could not get it. As he watched the hammer swing for his head, he used his whole body to jump right. Using his left arm, which had healed, he took hold of his knife, and before the Kappa could pull his hammer back from the ground, Rectify jumped and pierced his windpipe with the blade. Instead of seeing blood spluttering from the wound, he saw a strange putrid liquid. Quickly jumping around to the back of the Kappa, he ripped it's helmet off with his right hand, revealing a bulbous head that definitely wasn't human.

Clearly angry, the Kappa tried to make noise but could make no sounds beyond a gurgle. Dropping the hammer, it reached for it's neck to try and staunch the flow. Rectify quickly retrieved his sword and began walking backward to Koukai and his men, continually keeping his eyes on the Kappa. He was sure the Kappa could also heal, though probably not as fast as he could. It turned it's cold dark gray eyes on Rectify. It pulled a short sword from a scabbard built into the armor, which Rectify had never noticed until now, and it started coming for him, though not as fast as before. Based solely on his walk, he was scared.

Hoping to end this fight, he taunted the Kappa.

"Clearly, if you can't beat the lesser version of me, you never had a chance against the old me." Turning his back to Yertle, Rectify walked toward Koukai, knife in his left hand and sword in his right.

Taking a few steps, he felt the Kappa charging to kill him. Just before the short blade could pierce Rectify's heart, his sword knocked the Kappa's sword to the side. In the same motion, he jumped, stabbing his knife down through the top of the Kappa's head, dropping it to it's knees, more vile liquid oozed from it's head. Rectify stood before the disarmed, dying Kappa.

"I've killed many men I can remember, and perhaps many I do not remember as you've told me." Rectify put his knife away. "You know when Abel," the Kappa made a grunt at the mention of Abel. "So you recognize the name, makes sense, I guess," he shrugged. "Obviously, he didn't tell me everything, especially after I told him I was tired of killing. But for some reason, I don't have that feeling with you, hmm; I suppose I could let you live. Tell me, Yertle, if I allow you to live, will you join me in my endeavors?"

The still speechless Kappa raised his head looking at Rectify, then bowed his head to show he would serve him. Rectify was surprised, but given his experiences thus far, he didn't believe the Kappa.

"You surprise me, you would join me in killing your brothers and those like you?" Rectify looked intently into it's eyes, trying to sense what it was thinking. He couldn't read his thoughts, but he still perceived the same dark, seething, unending hatred this being had for him.

"I know you lie, Kappa!" Rectify shouted for all to hear. "You would kill me the first chance you got and break your word just as Koukai. Without honor, you are nothing, and I know you hope I will talk long enough to give you time to recover. I will provide you with only one thing."

Without hesitation, he took his sword in both hands and sliced the Kappa's head off, to the sound of a collective gasp from behind him. The head fell to the ground, the murky liquid pouring out. It's armor collapsed as its skin shriveled, leaving nothing but a puddle of armor, skin, and liquid, which quickly absorbed into the ground. Only it's head remained.

Turning, Rectify pointed his sword at a clearly confused Koukai, who obviously couldn't understand how this common man just killed a god.

"I have slain your god, and I will kill any that stand against me! I will give you only one chance to run, and it's now."

At first, nothing happened. The men looked back and forth at each other, then to his right a spear fell to the ground, and a man ran to the gates. From his left side, two more fell. Then suddenly, half the men from the right and left sides of the square were at the gate, throwing the doors open. The gates opened to reveal a state of chaos. The men fleeing from inside the fortress clawed and fought their comrades guarding Kaito's men outside in their haste. Seeing men running in such a panic, they too ran. No longer guarded, Kaito and the men from the farm came running with their weapons. Going up the five steps, the 10 men spread out in a line behind Rectify.

"I say it again if you wish to save any of your men, Koukai, you may face Kaito. I swear on my honor when you lose, I will allow your men to return to your father, though I will take everything from them first so your father will know of your shame."

Koukai stepped down from the large porch in front of the palace.

"Kaito can't even stand. How is he to fight me? Why should I even bother? I still have 10 men for every one of yours. Yes, I know you beat the Kappa, and yes, I am impressed," he waved his hand as if it was nothing. "He was the smallest of his kind, and clearly weak, so he is of no concern. The men that ran were not good soldiers. Alas," he said, motioning to all his men, "not all can be warriors of renown as these men are. Sadly, I must include trash with my great warriors." Raising his voice, he questioned. "What do you say, my mighty warriors, shall I waste your efforts and make you fight this pointless battle, or should I kill the cripple Kaito?!" The men shouted their obligatory agreement.

"It seems my men have spoken. Go fetch Kaito that I might take him out of his misery."

Koukai took a sharp inhale of air and stepped back, tripping over the porch, when he realized the man that took a step out of the line behind Rectify was Kaito.

Rectify stuck his arm out to make Kaito stop.

Rectify shouted to no one in particular, "You had your chance, men of Koukai, now face my wrath for I am Rectify!"

He didn't know where Sikanna and his men were, but hoped they were near and would know to attack with the revelation of his name. From around the walls, bodies fell, which surprised Rectify, first because he didn't know there were men on the walls and second because emerging from the shadows on the walls were the Ainu. There were about 10 on either side overlooking the courtyard with bows trained on the foe below.

CHAPTER 14
A LEGACY UNFOLDS

Sitting on the porch, Koukai's eyes widened in shock. He had just seen a being which he thought a god struck down by what he had thought was a man, but clearly wasn't. His hidden men who had been trained in stealth and secrecy by a man from these very Ainu were dead. He mocked Rectify, who must be a god himself and could've destroyed him at any time. Now a man, who should've been near death, strode forward in all his battle glory. For the first time in his life, Koukai understood the meaning of fear, which he thought he was beyond.

He willed his body to stand, but his legs would not move, as though they knew there was no hope. He was Koukai and would fear no man or being for surely he was no mere mortal. He, too, was a god and still outnumbered his enemy. Most importantly, in Koukai's mind, he was of rare intelligence; no other person, not even his father, much less a god, could match his genius. Full of confidence he stood; if he could not win the day with martial prowess, he would win by cunning alone.

He strode forward, displaying an air of complete confidence that his men may see they had nothing to fear.

"What manner of evil trickery is this, for how could Kaito have been injured so grievously and now stand as though he has no injury. I will tell you why because we have been deceived; this Rectify is a liar. First, you come here claiming your name is Yuuto, but now you're revealed as a liar, and further exposed for the man you came in with before could not have been Kaito. To defeat one of the great Kappa, you must be a demon, a child spawned of darkness. How can I be expected to keep my word to one so false?"

Snapping his fingers, the doors of the palace burst open, and out came four women held by two men each. Kaito and Rectify, who had both been walking forward, stopped at the sight of Hana, her two ladies, and Rectify's Ainu sister with swords to their necks.

Koukai beamed. Once again, his significant intelligence had prevailed. He pointed at the women.

"What is this? Are these the precious women the two of you are here to save? How unfortunate they must see your demise. Yuuto, Rectify, whatever your name is, it matters not, you boasted you can kill all of my

men. So far, you've only proven yourself to be a liar and lacking in honor. I

am a man of integrity, and I have given my word that I would fight Kaito to

the death, which would be no difficult feat but, I do not believe you will

honor your word, Rectify..."

Rectify knew all the things he said were false and wanted everything to

seem as human as possible. With the women now in play and his anger

growing, it was time to adapt his strategy.

"You speak to me of honor, yet you are using four women as

shields. Right now, you have 20 arrows aimed at you. There is no way you

can win. Within one minute after you die, all of your men will be dead.

Surrender now, save your men, and in the name of honor fight Kaito!"

"Ha, fool! Rectify, do you actually think you can outwit me? The

first arrow that flies will mark the death of these women. You are weak, and

therefore without honor."

"Koukai, I will teach you the difference between weakness and

mercy. You call me weak because I will not harm the innocent or those

weaker than me, but it is mercy. That is why I did not challenge you. You

are weaker than me, and I see now that I must show you the error of your

ways." He looked around to the walls at the men holding bows with arrows notched. "My friends, put your arrows away and come down from the wall." Rectify called

At this point, Koukai was sure the man before him was insane, for there was no way he could match 100 well-trained soldiers. But not everyone is fortunate to be blessed with his superior intellect.

"Very well… Rectify, prove you are not weak. Prove you have honor and defeat all of my men, show you don't make empty boasts. As I am a man of integrity, if you prove honorable and defeat my men, I will fight Kaito."

Sikanna and Kaito stepped forward in almost perfect unison to protest this clearly unfair task. Rectify raised his arm with his hand flat to stop them before they could speak.

"I can handle this, just keep your men back and make sure Koukai doesn't escape or harm any of the women."

Fixing Koukai with a steady gaze and clenched jaw, Rectify pointed his sword directly at him and shouted, "After I've killed all your men, you die next."

Koukai was shocked Rectify accepted his challenge, but it was not his fault if a fool truly believed in honor He turned, walking behind the women at the same time waving his hand, telling his men to kill. Immediately every spear was pointed at Rectify, every man moving back a spear's length. Men peeled from both sides to make one line behind him.

No one moved for several heartbeats until Rectify took his sword in both hands and leaped into the middle of the ranks in front of him. The enemy could not possibly have prepared for an attack such as this. Their spears were useless in their bunched formation; the enemy's rearmost rank lost five of their men in one sweep of curved death. In the chaos, 10 more were eliminated. All thoughts escaped from Rectify's mind. He was in the midst of a battle song, but more balanced than the most perfect music. Every ally watching was amazed at the fluidity and perfection of the swordsmanship before them.

Kaito, who knew he was an excellent swordsman, was shocked at what was occurring before him. Though he did not understand what Rectify was, he knew he was no mortal. His sword, combined with his strength, cut through multiple spear shafts per slice.

As Rectify fought, he wasn't Dan Campbell or Yuuto; he wasn't even Rectify. He was justice, and it would be delivered to Koukai. To those watching, it was something they would never be able to forget. For those on the receiving end, it was more frightening than their worst nightmare.

Not only was he moving faster than any man or beast they had ever seen, but that sword seemed evil to them. It moved so quickly in his hands that it was a circle of lustrous death. Many had fallen, some surrendered, but Rectify was still surrounded by enemies. After surviving his encounter with the Kappa, he was smiling, knowing these men couldn't hurt him.

His sword could cut through their spear shafts and dented swords, but many had clubs and various blunt weapons he could not cut through, and they managed to hit him a few times. They were easily shrugged off but were enough to feed the enemy's confidence.

Rectify turned to one enemy sliced upwards, barely noticing the blood in the air as he turned to the next man cutting down to the same effect. The fallen under his feet were getting in his way. As his senses began to return, he couldn't understand why these men were still fighting. He reached out with his feelings to understand what was fueling his enemies' eagerness to die. He became aware of men standing behind them, waiting to slay any that tried to flee. Something told him that wasn't what made them fight with such fierceness. He could sense great fear, but he wasn't the source.

Then he felt a familiar feeling which he had observed and even felt himself so many times. It was fear that only comes from those fearing the loss of a loved one, whether it be a child, sibling, spouse, or parent. Not the fear of losing them to death, but the fear that comes when they are taken or lost, their fate never to be known. Each man surrounding him was oozing this fear. Stretching his feelings as far as he could, and sensed that the men he fought had this same fear, from some, he heard sister, wife, or mother. Each man fighting had a member of his family held captive by Koukai and threatened with death should any man refuse to obey.

The realization came that those who fled did not have this same security system in place, which is why they ran. None of these men save those holding the spears to their backs wanted to be there. He felt his anger grow; he always worked not to get angry because, as he well knew, that was when mistakes happen. Imaging himself in the same position, he would kill anything or die any death to save them.

He was so tired of dealing with the scum of the earth, and Koukai was the same. By now, he was unaware of his surroundings, not even aware that he had stopped fighting or of the men surrounding him backing away. He didn't feel the temperature rising or see the grass began to curl and smolder beneath him. Everyone, including his allies, was unconsciously stepping away from him. The heat was intensifying around Rectify, and those closest could feel a vibration. Rectify stared at the ground silent through all this until a sound began to emanate from him. It started low but grew in intensity. Only those who had heard the sound of an earthquake, volcanic eruption, or typhoon had heard anything similar. Any of those not wholly convinced Rectify was more than a man could no longer doubt.

His head jerked upwards, and he looked directly at Koukai. Koukai shrank away, unconsciously covering his eyes with a forearm because Rectify's eyes glowed white when they first opened. Koukai then dropped to his knees when Rectify shouted, "KOUKAI!"

The shout echoed off the walls, shook weapons out of firm hands, and was heard as far away as Kaito's farm. It was felt by some who had heard it long ago and knew it was Rectify. All who heard it were filled with fear, especially those who had heard it so long ago.

Rectify's voice, though not as loud as when he shouted, still maintained its soul-shaking intensity.

"Koukai! Look at me, you scum of existence. I know the thoughts of your heart, and I know the feelings of your men. They only fight because you are a coward with no honor, and you have their loved ones held hostage. I hate your kind! You and the men who follow you have forfeited your lives, and I'm here to collect!"

With no warning whatsoever, the men holding those fighting at spear point so they could not run, dropped dead. A few who had been fighting fell, but more than that number thought dead stood. All who had fought for Koukai fell to their knees, bowing to the ground facing Rectify with their weapons placed before them. Koukai, now stripped of all pride and importance,

visibly shook and begged Rectify not to kill him.

His voice back to normal, Rectify laughed.

"Unlike you, I have honor; therefore, I cannot kill you, but you are

not worthy of fighting Kaito. Therefore, you must fight one who you do

not even consider a person. You will fight a woman."

Koukai began to laugh.

"A woman? I cannot fight a woman, for there will be no honor

when I kill her."

During the exchange, Kaito and Sikanna released the women who stepped

around either side of Koukai to return to their men. Save one, when Rectify

stopped his sister and motioned for her to come to him.

"No, Koukai, there will be no honor when you kill a woman

because she will kill you with my sword."

"What the Ainu woman? I was taught the secrets of the Ainu by

one of their own."

This got all the Ainu's attention, especially Sikanna, who rushed forward,

begging to be the one to kill Koukai. Rectify's sister claimed the right to

fight him as it was her husband that betrayed the family and taught their secrets. If anyone deserved to kill Koukai, it was her.

Rectify handed his sister his sword.

"Koukai, I would like you to meet the wife of the traitor who taught you the secrets of the Ainu."

That revelation clearly surprised Koukai. Smiling, he took his sword and walked towards the Ainu woman who he knew he could kill, and then he would take that curved sword and kill Rectify.

All backed up to give the combatants room. Then Koukai rushed forward without warning to quickly end such a foolish fight. He was shocked when the Ainu woman parried to the side, tripping him as he moved past her. Koukai stumbled, but was able to recover before his opponent could capitalize. Koukai became more conservative, but his opponent never changed her demeanor in the least. Every attack launched was evaded or parried. Everyone was amazed, save Rectify, who was proud of his sister. He just wished he knew her name. She had a natural talent and the skills she learned from her Ainu heritage. Rectify taught her a few extra tricks he doubted anyone else living knew, so he had no worries at all.

It was apparent Koukai had never gone this long in a sword fight. He was always allowed to win in his sparring matches, which he did not know until realizing he could lose to this woman. He tried to attack harder and faster.

but succeeded only in tiring himself as he moved slower and slower.

Koukai, now on the defensive, kept falling back until he was within 5 feet

of Kaito and Hana. Standing there, his sword in front of him, he was

obviously determined to die before he surrendered. Rectify's sister stepped

forward for a final strike when the sword fell from Koukai's hands.

Everyone stopped in shock until they realized that Hana's foot was now

visibly sticking out from between Koukai's legs. All the men visibly cringed

as Koukai slumped to the ground, but before anyone could take his life,

Rectify stepped in and ended the fight.

"Well, that was a surprise, but he is not worthy to die an honorable

death, and we must use him as a tool because his father is coming with an

army."

Hana did not like this announcement and begged to kill Koukai. They

found out he had killed her brother, and her sister-in-law died because they

were pulled away from her after the child was born. One of the ladies ran to

the room when they were freed and now held the baby, who was now the

new Lord of the land if he survived his ordeal. Due to his age, Hana would

be his surrogate mother and rule in his stead until he came of age. An

action which, much to his sadness because he wanted to be a farmer, made

Kaito the warlord.

Everyone seemed to be stunned to inaction until Rectify took charge.

"We must send messengers to all the neighboring lands. Tell them the rightful Lord has been slain by the hand of Koukai, the son of his father (somehow they always heard the name). Their infant son, now orphaned, calls on all who are loyal; his Uncle Kaito and Aunt Hana are now his protectors. Tell them Kaito is now the warlord of this land, and all are called to fight under his banner, for an enemy army comes that will kill their women and children."

The messengers left, leaving everyone there with nothing to do but prepare for the coming battle, which was only days away. If all lived, the Ainu would be given the farm and some surrounding land, as Kaito and Hana would now live in the palace. Funerals were conducted, and most of those who had served Koukai swore to follow Kaito in hopes that they would be able to rescue their loved ones. The others stayed behind; fearful their family would be killed if they were seen alive.

They shaved Koukai's head and dressed him in rags to present him to his father, as an insult to his so-called honor. They were determined to end the evil of Koukai and his father now. Hana took over the palace with exactness, and Kaito prepared for a military campaign. They asked Rectify to lead, but he declined, stating he was only there to help. He did direct the Ainu with scouting efforts. Rectify could see almost everything without scouts, but in the back of the enemy army was blank space, where it could have only been more Kappa.

Kaito and Hana created two units for special assignments. The first was led by Sikanna, and they were a mixed unit of swordsmen and archers who served as the Royal Guard. The other, to Rectify's surprise, was headed by his sister, but they hadn't determined a name yet. They only knew it was for subterfuge and intelligence.

CHAPTER 15
THE FIRST OF MANY BATTLES

It had been a week, and the enemy's army was now less than a day away

from the city. Rectify and his Ainu scouts had done an excellent job of

knowing where the enemy was and killing enemy scouts so t the enemy did

not know how many were with Kaito. Rectify was impressed with how

many people gathered to fight for Kaito and Hana. However, he was mildly

disappointed at the weapons and armor or lack thereof, the people showed

up with. The forces of Koukai's father were more numerous, probably by

several hundred, and they were better equipped for battle. Beyond the

numbers and equipment, this wasn't even half the army. The other half was

several days behind, but Rectify didn't tell anybody that part. No one

questioned the extra boxes of weapons, bows, and armor he somehow

found in the fortress.

He wasn't supposed to lead, but it didn't mean he couldn't assist. He also didn't tell anybody that he still couldn't sense what was at the back of the army. However, two of the Ainu scouts reported seeing at least two or three giants like the Kappa he killed in the fortress. He swore them to secrecy and assured them that he would deal with these Kappa. He spoke very confidently, and they believed him. Rectify wished he was as confident as they were. He barely beat the last one, and that was one-on-one. What was he to do with three or more? He had recognized a few of his abilities. Evidently, from what everyone told him about his confrontation with Koukai, he had powers he did not recognize. Apparently, when he got angry, he somehow manifested anger as heat.

He had spoken with Abel about it, but as usual, Abel wasn't very informative. All he said was. "Oh, you'll figure it out..., Remember you don't have to ask for permission to do or make what you feel is right." Rectify's favorite was, "remember controlled anger is a valuable tool." He guessed he could make things happen that were out of the ordinary and could do things when he got angry, and if he controlled it, it would be even more powerful. He tried not to dwell on it too much, just hoped it would work out.

He was nervous, he hated to admit it, and a little scared. With every mission he had ever been on, there was always some worry, anticipation, and fear of possible death. Looking back, when he did die, it wasn't as bad as he thought it would be. The adrenaline had been there long enough that he hadn't really felt much pain, just the fear of leaving his parents and Sonya behind. Up until his fight with the Kappa, when he found out how much rested on his shoulders, he hadn't been worried. Knowing that he could die and countless others would too if he did, increased his fears. Now he was possibly going to fight more… He just hoped he could beat them. He was pulled away from his thoughts when one of his Ainu scouts in a sweat came running, reporting that the enemy was 4 hours away.

Rectify stood from the desk he was sitting at, reached for his rifle, laughed, and remembered it was a long time away. He made it a point not to wear armor for the fight he knew he was to face. For one thing, it would make him stand out, and second, his enemy would be wearing heavy armor. Not wearing any would give him that much more of an advantage. With the weapons they were hefting, no armor would protect him. He was actually glad the battle was about to start; in the time it took them to prepare and gather soldiers he had taken to the desk for administrative tasks. He hated this part of military life. If he had his way when he was serving, he would never have gone beyond Major because he didn't like paperwork.

He was just about out the palace doors when his Ainu sister approached them from the side excitedly. This was going to prove interesting, he thought as he had never seen her show any kind of excitement about anything.

"Brother... Rectify..." she said hesitantly; he had been trying to get her to call him by his name, though he didn't yet know her's. "Lady Hana has decided to name my unit after me!"

"That is quite an honor. I am happy for you. But I do not even know your name. How does she know your name to be able to name the unit after you?"

"That is easy; she does not know my true name, and I can just call my unit whatever name I choose, but perhaps it will be my name. Rectify. I'm ready to tell you my name." She paused, and just as she started to tell him, Kaito entered the palace.

"Rectify, the time of battle is upon us. The men are assembled in front of the palace gates waiting for you to address them."

"Wait... me? Why me? You are the warlord and the commander, I am just..." Before Rectify could say more, he was cut off by Kaito.

"Just? You are the man who single-handedly killed the Kappa, who you once laughed away as a superstitious legend. You were the only one who could've defeated it, no one else could. You have been sent here by the gods, and you are the one who will save us all. If you do not address the men, they may leave."

Rectify forgot he wasn't dealing with trained soldiers, but peasants. He had

actually helped train them himself and should have paid closer attention to

their whisperings to each other. He asked people not to tell what had

happened in the courtyard, but secrets rarely stayed secret.

"Yes, yes, I guess I better go speak to the men."

He turned to go out the door when he remembered his sister was about to

tell him her name. He turned to speak, but she told him to go address the

men, and she would talk to him after the battle.

"Of course, after we defeat this enemy, we will talk." *That is if I can

kill the other Kappa,* he thought to himself.

Standing before the men on top of the gate, he had to take a breath. All

down the street and in every open area, the men stood, craning their necks

to see him. He couldn't help but smile. Watching old movies, it had always

been his dream to stand in front of soldiers holding spears and swords and

address them as their commander, now he got to do it for real. He just

hoped he could figure out what to say. He tried to think of every historical

person that had ever given a rousing military speech. He had a little bit of

Winston Churchill, Braveheart, George Washington, Patton, and a few

other notables going through his head. Finally, Kaito elbowed him so he would start.

"Men, I thank you for accompanying Kaito and myself into battle. You are here by choice; no one forced you to be here. Or have they? Marching towards us now is the army of Koukai's father" (which the men heard as whatever his name was.) "They have killed a good, honorable man, the Lord of this land, and not only him but his wife, and if not for the Lady Hana, his son, your new Lord!"

"I say no one has forced you to be here, but I am wrong you have been forced to be here because someone seeks to destroy your freedom and safety. Under Kaito and Hana, you will be governed by honorable people who will give you your just due. If you do nothing, a man who will defile your wives and enslave your children will become your Lord. If any man among you wishes this to be, let him be silent, but if you will fight, follow us, and let your voice be heard!"

Every man there shouted as loud as they could until Kaito held his hand up to silence them.

"We must defend our land! A ruthless enemy comes now to take it all away, but we will stop him! Our names may or may not be known throughout history, but you and the man who fights beside you will know in every life and throughout the eternities. You and they will see when you stay true, and all will know you fought with honor. Some of us will die, but for those of us who die, shall never be forgotten, and your sons and their sons will grow into great men because they will know their father died an honorable man because he died for them. For those with no sons, you will live on through the tales your comrades tell of your bravery."

"You have my pledge that I will not run, and I will not surrender. I will fight like a dragon to keep as many of you alive as I can. Whether you live or die, know I have done all I can to fight for you. I only ask you to fight as I do. The enemy may outnumber us, but they do not have our hearts and our just cause."

"Now, we could stay here and talk all day, or you can follow Kaito and I into battle. We each have our own fight this day. You must follow Kaito and know any command he gives must be obeyed. I wasn't going to tell you men, but I know you have heard the story of how I defeated the Kappa. It is true." He waited a few seconds for the gasps and shouts of excitement to ebb.

"There are more in the enemy army, but I will defeat them with your help. While I am fighting them, I need all of you to keep the rest of the enemy army busy. Indeed, I am not like you and have been sent here by the gods, but this enemy can kill me." Suddenly all breathing stopped. "I do not fear because I know we will win! No enemy can stop us, be they man or demon because we fight for JUSTICE!"

Finishing his speech, he jumped down in front of the men to be at their level. Taking a battle standard from one of the men that he recognized as having Kaito's symbol, he raised it in the air as Kaito came down to join him and once again shouted. "What do we fight for?"

In unison, the men shouted, "JUSTICE!"

Sikanna, his sister, Hana, and a few others joined them in front of the men, along with a bound. shaved Koukai and a bag containing the head of the Kappa. Rectify took the flag and began waving it as he ran back and forth in front of the men, shouting justice over and over, to which the men joined. He told Kaito he wanted to lead the men on foot while Kaito led them on a horse because Kaito was the army's leader.

As he roused the men, the horses were brought out, for Kaito, Sikanna, Rectify's sister, and a few other prominent leaders from neighboring towns. In addition, there was one for Rectify. Just as they had rehearsed, Rectify returned to the army's front, where he publicly said he would not ride as he would march with the men, receiving another cheer. The leaders set forth on their horses, and then retaking the banner, Rectify shouted for all to follow him.

After a few hours of marching, they arrived at the place where they had planned to defend against the larger army. To one side there was a slight hill which would give archers a height advantage, a river in front of them which was the same river they had to cross to reach the city. Rectify was excited yet nervous. He was practically jumping. He was excited for the coming struggle, it had always been his dream to fight in such a battle, but now that it was here, he realized it would probably be more like a nightmare. All were seated or lying on the ground, waiting for the enemy to arrive. All save Rectify, who stood at their front, holding the battle standard, wearing a simple farmer's hat to block the sun from his eyes and obscure his face, if necessary.

The men tried to nap or whispered amongst themselves of family and the glories of the coming battle. Each man was careful to avoid the thought on each mind that this might be their last day of life. Rectify listened to the men talk and smiled. It seemed that regardless of the time or the culture, people were more similar than they were different. He imagined the same thoughts and feelings had occurred beginning with the cavemen and would continue the same even beyond when he died. He remembered his disgust with war and how ironic it was that he had seen so much, and even after he died, he was still on a battlefield. How stupid war is, everyone can be at peace, but it just takes one person to ruin it all and make war necessary.

He reflected on the reasons he had fought. They weren't so different from why these men fought. He fought for his family, freedom, liberty, justice, and above all, peace. As thoughts again began to drift to Sonya and the dreams, he once had of being at peace and being married to her, he quickly redirected them to other things. He took some time to talk to Abel in his mind. He got a few more details about who he was and who these Kappa were, but not much.

It was strange it happened in another life, but somehow, he couldn't remember it. It was also odd he didn't remember it or remember those he was protecting, but somehow, he had the feeling he wanted to do it. Abel wouldn't tell him any names just that he had only met a few of them as Dan Campbell, and he wouldn't meet them all during his missions as Rectify. The most confusing, even disturbing, part was that Abel insinuated there was someone he would want to protect even more than Sonya. *But how could that be? I could never love anyone more than Sonya. Sure he loved his mom, but that was different.* He played it off, assuming Abel was just using some kind of misdirection to keep him on task.

Abel quickly left that conversation for what was at hand. He said it wasn't to keep secrets, but was what was best for Rectify. Rectify wasn't sure if he really believed that, but he wasn't going to voice his opinion. He found out there were not two or three Kappa, but five accompanying the enemy army. Abel was sure Rectify could defeat them all with the things he had learned in the last fight and what he unleashed when he got angry. Abel reminded Rectify to not let his thoughts hold him back, but to unleash them and try anything that came to his mind.

Apparently, all humans are capable of doing much more than they do, but it is the limitations they place on themselves that hold them back. All the stories of mothers lifting cars off of their children were less because of adrenaline and more because, at that moment, they did not let their human thoughts hold them back. Other than details about the enemy troops' composition and relevant information about their leaders, he didn't tell much more. Rectify only really listened to the part about the Kappa. There were creatures like them worldwide in many forms. They were all his enemies and were continually looking for signs of Rectify.

The dust from the enemy army was visible long before any soldiers were actually seen. Kaito was the first to draw anyone's attention to them and didn't have the men stand until the enemy leader was visible. The enemy had been marching in a column, and when they saw an army on the other side of the river, they began to spread out. Rectify was actually impressed with the fluidity of their formation change. He had to give them credit. Their men may not have been fighting by choice or out of any love for their commander, but they were well disciplined.

The leaders of both armies gathered across the river from each other, both warily watching the other. With both sides arrayed for battle, it was apparent to everyone the enemy had more men than Kaito and Rectify. Rectify was pleased to look back and see that none of the men were showing fear or trying to leave. Instead, they were looking expectantly at him as though they could not lose when they were on the side of Rectify. Rectify just wished he had a Rectify to look to for that same confidence. He guessed that since Sonya had given him confidence in every other battle, she would do so now because he was still doing this for her.

The last to walk to the army's front were five men if you could call them that, taller than any of the mounted men, and three were easily larger than his old friend Yertle. The other two were close enough in size that it didn't matter. As of yet, they didn't know which man in the army was Rectify but were obviously looking by the way they scanned the army. Rectify hoped pulling the hat down over his face would keep them from knowing it was him until he was ready for them to know.

Finally, someone from the enemy army shouted across the river.

"My Lord ..." (this whole not being able to understand specific names was getting annoying.) "Demands you remove yourselves from before his great army. As surely, you must know his son now rules this land under his most honorable and noble father. When you remove this rabble from before this great army, my Lord will allow you to live." Then the man laughed. "Do not remove them, and you will all die."

Not a single man moved. "My Lord will allow your leaders to come forward to surrender." He waited expectantly.

Finally, Kaito and Sikanna moved forward on their horses, pulling a shaved and nearly naked Koukai behind them with the sister, Rectify, and three others following from behind like they were servants.

Koukai was pushed forward and fell to his knees with his hands tied behind his back and gagged. Kaito dismounted, walked behind Koukai, removing his gag and cutting the cords holding his feet. Then resting his sword on Koukai's shoulder, he spoke.

"You can tell your Lord, I am Kaito, I've already killed one of his sons, and I hold another son's life in my hands. His first son died worthily in single combat. This being which he calls his son has no such honor and was defeated in single combat."

The speaker wasn't sure what to say, but a man who was actually wearing armor that had a samurai look rode up next to him on his horse. Obviously, this was Lord whatever his name was, and judging by his face, he was not happy.

"YOU! You kill my first son, and now you lie to me. I do not know what trickery you play or by what vile tricks you've used to entrap my son,

but it will not stand. I demand you show me the man who supposedly

defeated my most honorable son."

Kaito and Sikanna both glanced at each other with smiles in their eyes. It

was Kaito who spoke.

"I am afraid that is impossible."

"What? Do you refuse, or after my son defeated your champion,

did you capture and mistreat him?"

Kaito struggled to stifle a laugh. "I cannot present you with a man

who defeated your son, for he was not defeated by a man."

Rectify was only half paying attention to the exchange concerning Koukai

because he was watching the five Kappa. They had been scanning all of the

soldiers, obviously looking for who it was that defeated their brother.

When Kaito told it was no man, the five figures stopped and turned

towards Kaito in unison. It was clear to Rectify they knew he was the one

that killed their brother and then expected this to be the moment when he

would be revealed. They returned to scanning, after Kaito informed the

Lord that his son had been defeated by a woman, at which point the Ainu

sister walked forward.

The Lord was incensed. "WHAT? Do you dare insult me?! My son could never be defeated by a woman."

"I assure you it is true," Kaito replied.

The Lord snorted. "If this is so true, then I demand you give my son his weapon that he may fight this... Woman," he said as though she were less than an animal.

Sikanna threw Koukai's sword to his sister, who caught it with one hand. Rectify had to admit that was pretty impressive, and he certainly didn't teach her that. She walked to the side of Koukai and dropped his sword in front of him. She then walked behind him and cut the bonds at his wrists. She further made another move showing a side of her Rectify had never seen. Her arms crossed over her chest, she stood there with her back to Koukai, who now rubbed his sore wrists but seemed hesitant to pick up the sword until his father bellowed at him to pick it up.

Koukai retrieved the sword and hesitantly begin walking to the Ainu woman. Continually looking back to his father, he raised his sword when he was within striking distance, but hesitated. Hands still crossed over her chest, she turned. Koukai dropped his sword, leapt back, fell to his knees, and began begging her to spare his life. She walked away, never drawing her sword, as Koukai begged for his life with his head down. When he looked up next to the river, there was no one there. He left his sword and hurried across the river as swiftly as possible.

The enemy Lord shook his head and didn't know what to say for several moments.

"Perhaps my son is not the man I thought he was, but no matter, I have other sons, and I can make many more. I will take that woman and breed her like a cow."

Sikanna nearly flew from his horse to kill the man who insulted his sister, but she stopped him first. For the first time, she spoke.

"I need no man to defend or fight for me. I defeated your son twice, once for my husband's betrayal and now for myself. I do not fear you or any man. Send your champion if you wish, and I will defeat him as well."

At that moment, Rectify directed the staff with the Kappa's head attached to be uncovered and raised.

The Lord was clearly flabbergasted and had no idea how to respond to the revealed head, but more so to having a woman dare to speak out of turn to him.

"I will teach this insolent woman her place. She will not be so brave when my champion removes her head from her shoulders."

Her only response was to draw her sword and beckon with her other hand to the Lord to come forward. The Lord immediately pointed to a man and told him "kill that woman!" The soldier took two steps when a deep in-human shout made him stop and every head on both sides of the river turned.

The largest of the Kappa strode forward, and the enemy Lord bowed to him.

"Rectify, I know you are here! I know you got lucky against our brother, but he truly was the weakest of us all. In this form, you cannot hope to harm us. I don't know what your game is, but I will kill every last one of these humans until I find you if you do not show yourself. Surely you know by now that we can kill you, and you are not immortal. We have a power you cannot fathom. We know you have secreted archers to our flanks, which would be a masterful tactic if we did not know, and they could shoot in the rain."

Rectify and the rest of the men looked up to the clear stormless sky with confusion, but the enemy Lord and his men laughed. Not at the sky but at the confused faces of their opponents.

The five Kappa had their arms raised above their heads, and the water from the river began to ripple. Droplets started to move up to the sky as though it was rain, but in reverse, from all sides, dark clouds started to form, and a torrential downpour with strong wind began. The visibility was so low a man could hardly see past the length of his arm.

Rectify wasn't prepared for them to have this kind of power and knew he had to do something to counteract it, but he wasn't sure what. He was taking time to consider it when a sudden jet of water shot from the other side of the river and took out a column of men. Rectify had slightly better vision than everyone else, so he ran to the men to see what he could do to help, but the force of the water killed them instantly. Rectify drew his sword turned to the river and shouted a battle cry that wasn't loud enough to penetrate the noise, so the enemy had no idea.

Rectify would soon make sure he got their attention.

Abel, what can I do? How am I going to compete with this? But he heard no voice, only the memory he could do anything he saw fit. *I'll show these stupid turtles.* He raised his hands above his head and made a motion as though he were parting the clouds. At first, nothing happened, then all at once, a hole opened in the clouds directly over Rectify. Seconds later, a line of bright sunlight showed through the clouds as though a knife had cut the sky in half. Rectify threw his hat off, drew his sword, and walked to the river. The Kappa all drew their weapons in anticipation of the attack.

Holding the sword in his left hand, Rectify raised his right and made the motion of grabbing something with his hand and then quickly throwing it down. As soon as his hand reached the bottom of its imaginary strike. A ball of flame flew straight down from the sky into the river directly between Rectify and the Kappa. The result was a cloud of steam obscuring everyone's view.

Rectify took the sword in both hands and leaped through the steam across the river. Not even the Kappa expected that. His first slice was set to remove the leaders' head from his body, except he used his sword twice as thick and longer than Rectify's to block. Both blades slid down to the hilt, and the Kappa pushed Rectify back as far as he was tall. The leader walked behind the others and commanded them to kill Rectify.

Rectify stood sword at the ready, looking up into each of their eyes. None would make the first move, so Rectify, true to form, did the unexpected. He dropped his guard and started laughing, causing the Kappa and everyone else to look on in confusion.

Getting his laughter under control enough to speak. "I'm sorry, but you just don't know how funny this is. I've got the four of you here that all look like turtles. I just can't resist what I'm about to do."

He looked at their weapons. The first had a sword slightly smaller than the first Kappa's. The second a sizeable wooden staff with metal strips on it.

The third carried two axes that would each be considered two-handed axes

for a human, and the third was a mace with a spiky head on it.

"You with the sword, I'm going to call you Leonardo, wood staff,

you're Donatello, I guess Mr. ax guy you have to be Raphael, and you, are

you sure you can't use some nun chucks or something with a chain on it?"

The thing looked at him like he was the biggest idiot on earth. Rectify let

out a big sigh. "Fine, I'll call you Michelangelo. I hope you at least like to

party or something."

The Kappa clearly didn't know what to think. The leader of the Kappa

spoke from the back. "Rectify, you always did have the stupidest jokes.

You may think it's funny to mock us because we are nameless, but when we

kill everyone that helped you and show you real torture, we'll see what's so

funny. Now kill him!!!"

Raphael threw one of his gigantic axes with enough power to split an

elephant in half. Luckily Rectify was able to dodge in time. He recognized

that while he could evade and parry, his sword wasn't going to hold up long

against the strength of these things and their weapons. Remembering his

ability to make something become something else, he grabbed the battle-ax,

holding it next to his sword. He hoped it would work. In less than a second,

steel from the ax absorbed into his blade, the wooden shaft quickly discarded.

The one he named Raphael was clearly upset at the loss of his ax.

"How in the… did you do that?"

Just before dodging a devastating blow from Michelangelo, he retorted.

"I'll tell you if you tell me how you all have that kind of armor,

which is clearly far more advanced than should exist in this period of time?"

"Shut up Rectify! You always did talk too much, and you'll learn

soon enough after we defeat you, you will not die for a long time, and then

your pain will be so great you will forget such foolish questions."

After that, the talking was done

*

Kaito couldn't believe what he saw, but he couldn't look away like every

other person there. After watching Rectify fight the single Kappa, he really

wasn't sure even Rectify could defeat five by himself. His confidence was

bolstered when he saw the amazing feat with the ax and the sword. Four of

them had him surrounded, but for some reason, the fifth one, who was the

leader, still hung back, and from the looks of it, he may not need to help.

The larger sword was holding up well against the onslaught. At times all the weapons were coming at Rectify at the same time. None of the combatants

were giving an inch. These Kappa were obviously better than the other

Kappa. He could only imagine what it was like for Yu…Rectify. But if he

knew anything, he knew Rectify wasn't scared.

*

Rectify was more scared than he had ever been in his life, even more than

when that kid shot him in the gut. He was doing just fine against Leonardo

because while the sword was bigger than any he had ever fought against

before he had learned to fight against Kaito. He found the hardest part was

while the sword was predictable and fluid, all the other weapons were not

the same. Had it not been for his heightened senses, he wouldn't have stood

a chance.

Obviously, they were not used to fighting together, much less an opponent

who was a challenge. Yet somehow, they did have fighting experience. He

wondered who these things were because they had technology in their

armor and weapons that did not belong in this time. Much less in Japan.

Catching the wooden shaft of Michelangelo's mace Rectify shoved these

thoughts to the back of his mind. Just as he did with Raphael's ax, he

absorbed the metal part into his sword, making it bigger. Holding the

remaining wood handle with his left arm, Rectify used all his might to push

it away from him despite the Kappa using both arms to push it down.

Rectify pushed harder than he ever had in his life and couldn't understand why he was somehow overpowering something bigger and what should be stronger than him.

Still holding his sword in his right hand, he threw the wooden staff to the left, making Michelangelo fall forward towards the ground. In one swift motion, Rectify cut it's arm off, and quickly pulling his sword back, sliced once more, removing the Kappa's head. He didn't even have time to realize how bad the smell of the fluid coming out of the Kappa's body smelled, not as bad as a skunk, but like the worst flatulence ever. He would've noticed the smell had his shin not folded around the wooden staff of Donatello, completely shattering and folding his leg in on itself.

He felt dizzy and sick to his stomach, not just from the pain, but from the sound of his bones breaking. He knew it would heal. This was a terrible time for it to happen because if his healing was slow with Yertle, he had no idea how slow it would be with five of them. He didn't have time to hurt because of the ax that came down right where his head was.

*

Sikanna was amazed at Rectify's speed. From the time he first met him in the woods those few months ago, he was shocked to see how much faster Rectify was than him and was amazed he was even faster when he fought the first Kappa. Now he was even faster, and despite a broken leg which should've meant death for anyone in combat, he had no idea how he could've rolled away from that ax. Though Rectify was some kind of god or mystical being, a broken leg was a broken leg. Sikanna could only guess that when in this mortal form, he was bound by mortal frailties.

Those frailties were accentuated all the more by the loud grunts Rectify made every time he moved. He was still on the ground rolling, dodging, sliding, and scooting to avoid blows. The alarming thing was though Rectify had killed one of the Kappa, they watched the fluid flow towards the others and absorb into them, making them grow larger.

Rectify made it to his knees in time to block a downward slice from the Kappa with the large sword. He had no time to rest because he immediately had to throw himself back to dodge an ax cut. He almost made it unscathed, but his sleeve was cut open, and blood was trailed down his arm. Rectify was good, but if he did not get off the ground soon, he would die, and then they would all die along with him. The one with the staff tried to reach in and break the other leg, but Rectify launched himself to the side just in time. They were so close to defeating him, but Sikanna could not understand why the one in the back still didn't fight, but was glad because if he did, Rectify would lose. Suddenly Sikanna's hopes rose because Rectify started to stand up.

*

Donatello was really starting to get annoying. It was bad enough he broke

one leg, but he sealed his fate as the next to die when he tried to break the

other. First, Rectify had to get off of the ground. His leg didn't feel like it

was flopping around as much as it had been, so he decided it was time to

stand up and fight. Using his good leg, he launched himself upright. When

he put weight on his broken leg, things got a little dark, and he fell again

just as the wooden staff from Donatello swept through where his head had

been.

Chills and nausea were all Rectify felt for several seconds when he hit the

ground. Donatello was just a jerk; that's all there was to it. That opinion was

further amplified when the same Kappa brought his staff down in a

crushing blow. Rectify was able to catch it and slow it down when it hit his

head. Rather than his head smashing it like a pumpkin, it felt like when he

was a running back on the football field. When he broke through the

defensive line, a linebacker was there waiting, and their helmets collided.

Rectify decided enough was enough. Kicking the Kappa in the knee and not

letting his grip on the staff lessen. He was able to take the staff and use it as

a crutch to make up for his bad leg. Before any of the others could reach

him, he got to the side of Donatello, who was cradling a hyperextended

knee. Before cutting it's head off, he spoke for the first time since the fighting started.

"It's not so fun when it happens to you, is it?"

Rectify reveled in the fact that he had now defeated two out of five. His relief soon turned to horror when he realized the liquid coming out of the dead Kappas was being absorbed by the other three making them stronger. As they were getting stronger, he was feeling more feeble every second. He had to do something and knew from his previous experiences there was always an extra gear. He could only hope it held true this time.

He didn't know how, but he could feel his leg start mending faster as he focused on it. It still hurt to put weight on it, but he would be ok by using the staff as a crutch. It was now 3 against 1. The leader guy, who he decided to call Shredder, came forward to join the fight. Shredder's sword was much bigger than his, but there was still some metal he could take on the battlefield.

Raphael came running ahead of the other two, expecting to take him by surprise and knock him off balance. Rectify used the staff to pivot, swung his body around, and used it to pole-vault his good leg into the face of Raphael, knocking his helmet off. The dazed monster dropped to his knees, head falling forward. Now standing to it's side, Rectify sliced down to remove his head, but the Kappa moved. Rather than going through it's neck, the blade took off part of the front of his head. That nasty liquid was coming out of it's head, but not enough to keep it from getting back up.

Somehow despite the gruesome injury he received, Raphael hit Rectify in the abdomen with an uppercut that sent him sprawling to the ground, his crutch knocked just out of reach. The thing lurched forward, holding Rectify down with it's legs and clamping his massive hands around his neck. The wound in on it's head was still oozing vile liquid. In his struggles to breathe, the liquid, which tasted akin to rotten eggs, filled Rectify's mouth.

The other two Kappa began cheering for Raphael because he just defeated the foe, they hated the most. As the promise of defeat was inevitable, Rectify's thoughts flashed back to his life, mostly on Sonya. The scene he envisioned was when she gave him his knife… the memory hit him like a lightning bolt. With his remaining bit of strength, he found he was able to reach his knife. He stabbed the beast in it's belly and twisted, then bringing the blade up, the innards of the beast gushed all over Rectify.

Kicking the remains of his enemy off him, he stood and found he could put weight on his broken leg. Leonardo stood transfixed between the shock of seeing his companion killed, and his enemy survive. When the liquid from his brother began absorbing, he was hit with ecstasy, knowing he was getting stronger. Rectify didn't have time to see any of this because the hit to his stomach, along with the putrid taste in his mouth, made him throw up. In the process of throwing up, he saw Raphael's ax laying on the ground.

Shredder, however, turned and summoned the humans to bring him his secret weapon. Not wasting a second of opportunity Rectify, took the great ax and threw it with both hands over his head striking Leonardo square in the face. It was now 1 to 1. Rectify quickly picked up his sword, walked as quickly as possible with his still tender leg, and absorbed the ax into his sword. Rather than absorb Leonardo's sword, he picked it up with his left hand. With a sword in each hand, he turned to face Shredder.

Shredder had been bigger than the other four, to begin with, but now he was at least twice Rectify's height and was even broader than he had been before. Both swords up, Rectify walked to the enemy who still had his back to him. Suddenly the enemy turned, slicing a sword that was even taller than he was directly at Rectify's neck. Rectify instantly turned and blocked it with both blades. The borrowed blade in his left hand was cut in half, the other receiving a deep gouge, but it was still in one piece.

The sword sliced his left arm open to the bone, making it hang useless at his side gushing blood. In his haste to face, the enemy he had not paid attention to his footing. He went to leap at the Kappa, but Raphael was not completely dead yet, and he grabbed his broken leg pulling him back. Rectify quickly sliced down and finished the enemy this time. Shredder's gigantic sword was coming down straight at his head. Closing his eyes, he put the blade above his head, in what he knew was a useless attempt at blocking the sword and braced for his defeat.

*

Watching from across the river, the woman who was supposed to see Rectify as a brother panicked because she didn't care what was right, she was in love with Rectify. She could tell he didn't know the one Kappa was still alive and screamed when it grabbed Rectify's leg. With no thought, she unleashed an arrow piercing the giant Kappa in the throat. With a speed that only comes from methodical practice, she unleashed her second arrow as she said under her breath "I love you, Yuuto." The second arrow struck the beast in the eye, and this time he screamed as though he were in agony. Dropping his sword, he turned and ran.

*

Rectify felt the giant blade hit his sword and then felt the blade hit his head and cut the skin. He felt the warmth of the blood trickling down his face. After several seconds of wonderment, he opened his eyes to see the Kappa's sword had indeed hit him, but it was now discarded, and he was running away. He wanted to try and chase it, but knew there was no way he could catch it. He had no idea what happened, but he didn't have time to find out because the whole enemy army was running towards him. He quickly put his hand to his blade, repaired it, and turned it back to its proper state. The metal from the other weapons dropped to the ground in three separate clumps. Returning his blade to his belt, he ran and grabbed the gigantic sword, touching it with his hand he made it near to the same shape as his sword.

He knew he shouldn't have had the strength to wield such a ridiculously large sword, but then he was learning more about himself every day. Wielding the sword, he turned to face the enemy army. Upon seeing a man wield the Kappa's sword, the enemy army stopped in it's tracks, despite their officers angered shouts. One mounted rider charged forward, unmistakably the leader because of his armor. Swinging the blade, Rectify was only able to hit him in his armored shoulder, which didn't kill him, but he didn't survive the landing.

Half the enemy army dropped their weapons and dropped to their knees in surrender. For some reason, the other half started charging towards Rectify once again. He was set to take the enemy army on in what he knew would become a legendary battle when he heard a sound of many bows being fired from behind him. He instinctively dropped to the ground as arrows struck the men in front of him, completely taking the fight out of them.

Rectify was exhausted and noticed for the first time how horrible he smelled. He stood long enough for his men to come across the river before he collapsed to the ground, passing out.

CHAPTER 16
END OF THE DREAM

Rectify's eyes opened to white walls and the sound of birds chirping. It took his eyes a moment to adjust and recognize he was back in what he guessed was now Kaito and Hana's fortress. He had been dreaming, at least he thought it was a dream, but he had gone to visit with some of his ancestors for a few hours. No, it wasn't a dream because he's Rectify. He woke up completely naked, covered by a sheet. Alone in the room, he noticed a change of simple farmers' clothes. Next to those in a corner was a pile of the clothes, weapons, and armor he had gone into battle with. Next to those were his boots, which looked like sandals to everyone but him, all sliced up.

His observations were interrupted by the sound of many feet coming into the room. First into the room was his Ainu sister, followed by Sikanna, Hana, and Kaito. They each looked at Rectify in silence, and he back at them in equal silence. All bowed to Rectify, but after several moments they didn't come back up. They stayed silent to the point that it was uncomfortable. But in his typical fashion, Rectify had to say something.

"Please rise up and look at me. I don't suppose I got here or took my clothes off by myself. I hope I wasn't too much trouble." Every person in the room looked over at the pile of clothes, especially the boots, at the same time.

"Worry not, Brother, your sister and I took care of you, but we did have some trouble with your... sandals? They, uh, were not like what we're used to."

"Yes, I suppose they would be because I modified them a little with my abilities. I learned a lot in the last... how many days has it been?"

"Three days," responded Kaito.

Rectify's eyes grew large in surprise.

"Three days!? How? It seemed like only a few hours. Did I do or say anything strange during that time?"

It was his sister who spoke up.

"There were a few strange things you said. You said Glanpa a few times and a few other words in some strange language."

Rectify couldn't understand what he had just heard until he realized with a heavy accent, she tried to say the word, grandpa. So indeed, it wasn't just a dream where he talked to his grandpa

"You also said two words or names Love and Protector quite often along with the name Sonya, and said you loved them."

Them? He understood Sonya. If he knew her before he was born and was called Rectify before mortality, it made sense she would be called something else before Sonya. But why would he have said two names? If she was Love or Protector, who was the other? For the first time, the thought came to him that perhaps he was wrong about Sonya, but he quickly cast that thought out of his mind.

Before standing from the bed, Rectify made sure to clothe himself. Then he stood, and they all bowed to him again, so he bowed back.

"Please rise up. I have so many questions. First, why did my last enemy turn and run? He should have killed me with that strike to my head." He reached up to feel the perfectly smooth skin where he had been cut. "I closed my eyes ready for death, which did not come, and when I opened them, the enemy was running away."

All eyes turned to his Ainu sister. Her cheeks were slightly reddened by the attention.

"I am sorry, Brother, but I could not stand by and do nothing. I hope you are not upset with me." Rectify just looked at her with his mouth open.

"When I saw that monster about to strike you down, I didn't think, I just took action. I launched one arrow into his neck, which did not slow him down. With more speed than I can ever recall having, I fired a second arrow into it's eye, and that was when it ran in pain."

Rectify stared at her speechless and bowed directly to her for two minutes. When he looked up, everyone in the room was bowing to his Ainu sister.

"I don't know what to say, Sister. You saved my life and the life of many others. You see, he would not have completely killed me, but would have held me prisoner and tortured me as he killed all those I cared about. But tell me, why was the second arrow so much more effective than the first?"

"Embarrassed," was all she could say for some time. "I cannot tell you now, but perhaps I will at another time."

Hana, cut in.

"For what she has done, we have appointed your sister, Kunoichi, as the leader of our secret guard. Her bravery and critical thinking will serve us in the future."

Rectify smiled

"My sister, I am pleased to know your name. Now, what else has happened in the three days I was unconscious?"

They all took turns telling him of the events he was unaware of. Many of the soldiers of the enemy army sought to join them after their Lord died. They executed Koukai for his dishonorable actions. Many more flocked to the fortress from the surrounding lands to swear fealty to Kaito. However, he did what all too few throughout history have been able to do. He denied the position and demanded they recognize his nephew as an Emperor. He and Hana were only his guardians.

The rest of the enemy army was on their way, and they were larger than the first. Now they were an equal match with all their reinforcements and another battle would again within days.

Kaito boldly announced the enemy army would be no match with Rectify at their head. Rectify was ready to accept the appointment with equal boldness. However, before he could agree, the feeling came telling him his time here was done.

"Wait, Kaito. I would like to continue to fight with you, but my time with you has come to an end. There are many others I must help."

"But Yuu... Rectify, surely your work can't be done, we need you!"

"Kaito, I know you will do well. It is time for all of you to forge a new future and your own destinies. I have given you all I can, rest assured we'll see each other again someday, and I will always be watchful of you, and should you ever need me again, I will be there."

Again, they all bowed to him. All promising that if the day ever came that he needed them; they would be there for him.

Now standing at the gate of the fortress, sword, and knife at his side. He did not want to leave. All around were sleeping soldiers because they thought it best Rectify leave at night. The only light in the sky was a bright moon, and as he walked, it seemed extra quiet except for what he thought were faint footsteps even he could barely hear.

He was headed for Kaito's farm, where he had first begun his journey. He didn't run as he could have or teleport. He wanted to walk. As he walked, he continued to hear the footsteps. Not until he got to the remains of the bridge, which already had wood and ropes for its repair waiting nearby, did he turn around and peer into the darkness, but saw nothing.

"Kunoichi, where are you?"

After a pause, he heard the sound of familiar footsteps. Then a small silhouette unfolded from the darkness, and it was indeed his Ainu sister.

"Rectify, I don't know what to say, but I couldn't let you go without speaking privately. You asked me why the second arrow had an effect when the first did not." She paused and swallowed. "As I drew my bow, I whispered... I love you."

Rectify had not expected this. He knew she cared about him and liked him, but did not think she loved him. He started to work his mouth and looked down, but it took several moments before words would form.

"Kunoichi, I- -"

But she stopped him.

"Please call me by my true name, Ninpo."

Ninpo's name struck Rectify as familiar, but he could no place it, nor did he spend much time thinking about it because he knew how sacred it was for her to give him her real name. She certainly wasn't making it easy for him to say goodbye.

He took a deep breath before placing his hand on her shoulder.

"Sister, no Ninpo, I am honored you would tell me your name, but I am sorry I must leave... And there is someone else I love far from here, another life really. I look nothing like the man you see, and my name then wasn't even Rectify, much less Yuuto."

She looked at him struggling to hold back tears.

"I know, you cannot stay, and I cannot have you but, may I see and know the real you, or the man who is true to the one he loves. I hope she knows how fortunate she is."

All Rectify could do was shrug his shoulders.

"I must warn you that where I come from, we look different from what you're used to, my name was Dan, but truly I am Rectify." With a thought, he turned back to Dan Campbell.

Ninpo gasped at how strange the man before her looked. He looked nothing like her Yuuto. He was light-skinned, his eyes a peculiar shape, and they were blue. But when she looked into his eyes, she could still see her Yuuto.

Rectify saw the expected response, but as she looked into his eyes, he knew she saw him.

"Rectify, I thank you for showing me the real you, but I have known the important parts of you all along. I tried to see you as a brother, but I cannot. You say there is someone else far away and, in another life, but if you stay, I promise to make you happy and be a good wife."

Rectify turned to her, his face full of care and sorrow.

"Ninpo, I'm sorry, but I can't stay, and you are destined for much more than to make a man happy and be a wife. You can make a man happy and be a good wife while living your own life. You have been given an important position that will have important impacts on the world and the future. I do care about you, and I certainly will never forget you, but you must remain my sister."

Ninpo looked back at him, a tear coming from her eye.

"I, I understand it was just a hope. But may I do something before you leave?"

Rectify wasn't exactly sure how to respond. He supposed with his leaving it was the least he could do.

"Go ahead."

Ninpo drew close to Rectify. He expected a hug or perhaps a kiss on the cheek. She did not hug him and moved as though she were going to kiss him on the cheek, but instead of kissing his cheek, she gently bit it. Surprised, Rectify stepped back and fell over a stack of wood. He was embarrassed! He quickly got to his feet, brushing himself off, then looked up and saw Ninpo was embarrassed too.

"I'm sorry about that. You surprised me. That's not really something we do where I come from."

"Oh, what do you do where you come from to tell someone you… love goodbye?"

"Well, I would give them a hug."

Ninpo gave a curious look.

"I have never heard of a hug. What is it?"

"It would probably make you uncomfortable, but you put your arms around the other person and squeeze. I can give you one if you would like."

Ninpo gave a very contemplative look.

"Though it sounds strange, I would like to try this hug."

Rectify put his arms around her, and she hesitantly put her arms around him, mimicking his actions. She did not exit the embrace as quickly as Rectify did.

"Thank you, Ninpo! Now I must be off, and you have things to do. I have a few things I need to do before I leave."

Rectify turned on his heel, making sure not to trip this time. He bent down and touched the part of the bridge anchored the shore. With the thought that he wanted the bridge completed, the materials on the bank disappeared, and the bridge was finished. He walked over the bridge, conscious Ninpo was watching his every move. Next, he walked to the tree, which had so graciously fallen over the river for him.

Placing his hands on the tree's trunk, he closed his eyes, thinking what he wanted the tree to hear. *I thank you for your help, but it is time for you to stand once again.* The up-turned roots began to reach for the ground, but the tree could not rise up. Rectify tried to use his strength and lift the tree. The place where he held his hands began to glow, and the tree slowly stood once again. With the tree looking as though nothing had happened, Rectify brushed his hands off on his legs. Then looking over at Ninpo, he waved, turned, and continued onto his destination.

*

Ninpo stood there until long after all trace and sounds of Rectify were gone. She looked at the bridge as she crossed it, amazed at what she had witnessed, and walked over to the tree which moments before was lying on it's side. Looking at the tree, she noticed the place where Rectify's hand had been. It was now a permanent scar the shape of his hands. She placed her hand in the scar, thought of Rectify for a few moments, and then laughed, thinking herself foolish to have thought he would stay for her.

As she walked back to the fortress, she thought of the coming future and her responsibilities. She wondered how they would change the future and determined she would do all she could to make Rectify proud.

*

Having reached the grove of trees where this adventure began, Rectify started to return back to Abel, but he couldn't.

"Hey Abel, what gives?

"You can only bring certain items here, you can bring your knife, but you have to leave the sword."

"What? My sword? I'm not going to just leave it here."

"Well, you don't have to leave it. You can find someplace to store it like a cave or something."

Rectify thought for a moment of what would happen to the metal in a cave. Then he thought of the Cheyenne base, which was built into a mountain, which gave him an idea. He remembered reading about these two guys from the Smithsonian Institute that discovered a cave in the Grand Canyon. He thought of such a place and instantly found himself inside a cave. He sat his sword against the wall. After making a few more adjustments and a way to hide the cave entrance, he returned to Abel's office.

Abel was sitting at his desk and looked up at Rectify as though he had been there the whole time.

"Rectify, your fascination with weapons is so strange, but I guess that's to be expected with your past and the things you've done. So, let's talk about that last mission and get you ready for your next."

Before Rectify knew it, he was leaving for his next mission.

THE AVENGING ANGEL

KEEP UPDATED!

Rectify is only the first series I will be writing; if you want to follow the exploits of Rectify or be informed of my current and future projects, text the word Rectify to +1 (928) 264-9413, and you will be able to connect with me personally and get all updates.

Email me at ryan@ryanjrussellbooks.com or find me on Facebook at https://www.facebook.com/RyanJRussellBooks.

I am grateful you've chosen to read this novel. The stories have been inside me for a long time, and I am glad to be able to share them with you.

I hope you will continue to follow the exploits of my friend Rectify, as you will next find him at the place all roads lead to.

I will try to respond to every message you send.

*

Love this book? Don't forget to leave a review!

Every review matters and it matters a lot!

Head over to where you purchased this book or places where it is sold, and

please leave a review.

Thank you very much!

ACKNOWLEDGMENTS

My Uncle Col. Dale Deloss Rowley, who you will read about in the book, most of what you read about him is real. He is a hero and part of my inspiration. He was one of the most decorated combat pilots in Vietnam.

I must also thank my dear friend and editor, RJL. I think you are an excellent editor, but even more, you are a wonderful friend.

I especially want to acknowledge Lon at Theory Forge Pro for the amazing covers. They are beyond anything I ever imagined

Last, but not least, thank you to the kind folks at Gila Valley Software for all their outstanding service and technical help.

ABOUT THE AUTHOR

Ryan lives in southeastern Arizona and thinks of himself as your average guy with Duchenne Muscular Dystrophy, who happens to have a Ph.D. in General Psychology and is an Eagle Scout. Ryan is a Life Coach and helps people change their lives, thrive with a disability, and prepare for old age.

He currently works with multiple charities. 10% of what he earns from the sale of this and future books goes to Operation Underground Railroad.

His current goal is to get a handicap conversion vehicle, which would significantly change both his and his parents' lives. 90% of what he earns from this novel goes to his vehicle fund and supporting himself and his parents.

THANK YOU TO ALL MY KICKSTARTER BACKERS

I couldn't do this without you.

Special thanks to those who contributed anonymously with no reward!

Avenging Angel Tier

Phyllis MacGilvray

Tucker Family

Justin John

Razorsoft, Inc.

Legendary Soldier Tier

Kristen

Beth Ann Russell

Dan Russell

Delta Force

Justin and Sheree Burrell

Charles S Pike

Navy Seal

Paloma y José Luis

Aaron Dodge

Kenny

Jadyn Hansen

Larissa Reed

Robert Sparks

Tyson Kempton

Connie McCurry

Carlene Barous

Major

Jerrold R. Shouse

LaWynn Brown

Lieutenant

Eric Hancock

Doris

Carrie

Don Marble

Trevor Sexton

Mike & Denise Cochran

James Carpenter

Gellianna

Jamie Allen

Onate Family

Early Bird Special Hardcover

Daniel Russell

Daniel James Nabor

Nicole Lunt

Zach & Shannon Brown

Becky Boone

Kambria

Chris Taylor

Delorse Woodside

Kas Jabbour

Callie Walters

Lieutenant, Junior Grade

Debbie Kempton

Kevin Thomas

Rick McBride

Early Bird Special Paperback

Tisha

Heather

Martha Bigler

Brant W Taylor

Megan Sieloff

Alex Larson

Traci Kempton Brimhall

Nicole Wood

Renshaw Family

Ensign

Matthew Demelio

Jacky

Mark Wahlbeck

Sergey Kochergan

Made in United States
North Haven, CT
04 April 2023

35032858R00157